THE INDOMITABLE HUMAN SPIRIT

PREPARATION

AKAANSHA ARNAB SENGUPTTA

Made with ♥ on the Notion Press Platform
www.notionpress.com

Dedicated to my family, for always supporting me <3

Contents

Contents

Preface

Hey there, It's me, A.S, get it? cause that was a trend circling around tiktok for a while? I'm writing this book to buy my brother a laptop since he plays fighting games on a phone and its really hard for me to see him do that. his old Ipad broke and since it's pretty old he couldn't get it fixed because there was no battery available. My hobbies are reading, horse-riding, archery, and creating fake scenarios In m head while I listen to music. This is one of them. Well, I wont keep you around for too long now, go enjoy the book.

Prologue

So, you're probably wondering, How on Earth did we end up in a galactic smackdown against aliens with God's personal blessing and a bunch of glowing percentages floating over our heads? Fair question.

Honestly, I was just as surprised as you. One minute, the UN is trying to figure out the Wi-Fi password, and the next, God Himself is like, "Hey, humans, you're about to face the intergalactic varsity team, but don't worry—I've got a plan."

Not just any plan though. See, God went all in with this one. Imagine you've been living your average human life, and suddenly, you get hit with a glowing percentage that tells you whether you're good at magic or physical combat (yes, we now all have RPG stats). If that wasn't enough to digest, you're told you've got 1,000 years to get ready for an alien invasion. Cool, right? Except we don't age during this time, and God has taken care of all our "earthly" burdens. You know, like taxes, pollution, and running out of ice cream.

Now, humanity is divided into two camps: the Foreground People (the battle-ready warriors) and the Background People (the brains, builders, and strategists). Both groups have to work together, which, as you can imagine, is like herding cats with laser pointers. Oh, and did I mention there are angels handing out special powers and family heirlooms like they're at a cosmic garage sale?

As for me? I'm Eleanor, and apparently, I'm the Greatest Dragon, a title that comes with fancy traits like Serpentine Sovereignty, Masterful Mage, and Ace Marksman. No big deal, right? Except that dragons—the greatest kind—were supposedly extinct, and now everyone, including the angels, are losing their collective minds.

But I'm not alone in this. My friends—Atticus, Delver, and Akuma—are powerhouses in their own right, leading factions like Serpent, Phoenix, and Avian. (Spoiler: Atticus is as gorgeous as I am strong. Try not to swoon.) Together, we've got 1,000 years to build armies, form alliances, and make sure Earth doesn't end up as alien lawn decor. No pressure.

Oh, and when the war finally comes after our millennia of prep? It's going to be one for the history books.

Let's just hope we're the ones writing those books.

CHAPTER ONE

So, God Hit the Reset Button.

Let me tell you something about being human: it was simple—emphasis on was. Go to school, get a job, pay bills, binge-watch something, rinse, and repeat. Simple, right? Yeah, well, that all went down the drain when a group of aliens decided Earth looked like prime real estate.

If I'd known an alien invasion was on the calendar, I probably would've skipped the extra slice of pizza last night. I mean, who wants to fight intergalactic overlords on a full stomach?

But that's exactly how the day started.

An alarm screamed at me, dragging me out of sleep like it was trying to rip the sheets off my bed. "ATTENTION ALL PEOPLE! WE'VE GOTTEN A DEVICE FROM THE ANGELS TO PUT A PERCENTAGE OVER YOUR HEAD! IF IT'S ORANGE, YOU'RE PHYSICAL; IF IT'S PURPLE, YOU'RE MAGICAL!"

I groaned and pulled my blanket over my head. Angels? Magical percentages?

I wasn't sure if I was still dreaming or if I'd fallen into some bad sci-fi novel. But nope, this was real. Apparently, the world's new pastime was figuring out if you were going to be throwing fireballs or flipping trucks. And I was about to find out which club I was in.

I stumbled out of bed, rubbing my eyes, and headed to the window. That's when I saw them. The crowd in front of the gate. Cops. Neighbors. And standing smack in the middle of it all—an angel. Yep, wings and all. Talk about a wake-up call.

Not one to miss the action, I threw on some clothes and ran downstairs. When I got to the gate, everyone turned to look at me, their eyes wide. The police officer waved me over like I'd just walked into some kind of reality show.

"Uh, angel?" The officer said, scratching his head. "Her percentage is 100."

One hundred? I barely registered it. He kept talking.

"And it says her blood type is 'Greatest Draconic,' with the traits Serpentine Sovereignty, Masterful Mage, and Ace Marksman. Is... is that good?"

Good? The angel's eyes practically bugged out of their head. "What? Let me see that. You probably got it wron—" He cut off and stared at me. I swear his jaw hit the ground. "Oh my God."

Now, when you've got an actual angel standing in front of you saying "Oh my God," you know something's up.

He blinked at me, then turned to the crowd. "She's the human race's jackpot! Greatest Dragon? That bloodline went extinct centuries ago! How is this even possible?"

I stood there, stunned. Jackpot? Greatest Dragon? I thought maybe I'd accidentally signed up for a lottery or something. But no, this was worse. Much worse.

"Wait!" The angel continued, "I have a family heirloom! It's an evolution stone for the Greatest Dragon. My family's kept it for generations, hoping we'd see one in real life!" The angel started rummaging through his robes like he was looking for his keys.

I blinked, and before I could react, another angel popped into existence. Like, just appeared. I hadn't even had time to process the first one.

"I heard what's going on. I brought the stone," the new angel said, holding up what looked like a glowing rock the size of a grapefruit. "Holy... that's an actual Greatest Dragon!"

"And guess what traits she's got," the first angel said, like this was some cosmic game show.

The second angel raised an eyebrow. "What?"

"Serpentine Sovereignty, Ace Marksman, and Masterful Mage."

That seemed to be all the confirmation they needed, because the second angel shoved the glowing rock into my hands. "Quick, evolve her."

"Wait, wha—?"

Before I could even finish, the stone flashed, and my entire body lit up like a Christmas tree. For two seconds, everything felt... right. Like I was floating, free of any worries or doubts. Then the light vanished, and I was back, standing on the street, everyone staring at me.

Except now? My hair was white. So were my eyelashes. My eyebrows too. Oh, and my eyes? Pink. I looked like a walking snowstorm with an attitude.

"Great," I muttered under my breath. "Because what I really needed today was a makeover."

The angels were nodding to themselves like they'd just solved world hunger. "She's ready. Fully evolved. The Greatest Dragon returns."

That's when it clicked. This wasn't some random Tuesday. I wasn't just Eleanor anymore. I was humanity's biggest shot at surviving the invasion.

And my family? They just stood there, wide-eyed, nodding, as if they had made peace with me joining the angels. For the greater good of the world, of course.

Perfect. Just perfect.

I'd been dragged into the cosmic lottery, and now I had a new title: The Last Greatest Dragon.

And the real kicker? I had to lead an entire faction—Dragon—into war. Because nothing says "welcome to adulthood" like becoming the leader of a magical army.

There's nothing like finding out you're humanity's "jackpot" to kick your day into overdrive. I didn't even get to process the whole Greatest Dragon business because before I knew it, people were swarming me like I was a celebrity who just walked into a sandwich shop.

One of the angels clapped his hands. "Alright, everyone, back it up! Give her space. She needs to get ready. We've got a lot of work to do!"

Work? My brain was still stuck on the glowing rock and the weird transformation. I looked down at my new snow-white hair. Honestly, I could get used to it—it had a kind of badass, mystical vibe. But still, work?

"Wait, wait, wait," I said, holding up my hands as the crowd started to back away. "What exactly does 'getting ready' mean? And why do I feel like I just got drafted into something?"

The angel (the first one, the guy who gave me the stone) turned back to me with a look that said, oh, you poor thing. "Well, Eleanor," he said, trying to sound casual, "now that you're the Greatest Dragon, you're the leader of the Dragon faction."

I blinked. "The what now?"

He raised his hand, and a hologram map of the world shimmered into view, right there in the middle of the street. If the neighbors hadn't been convinced we were living in a sci-fi epic, they were now.

"Look," the angel pointed at several glowing spots on the map. "There are four major factions humanity has been divided into. You'll be leading the Dragon faction, which is primarily magical. You'll be in charge of the ranged attackers, the heavy-hitters. Dragons go headfirst into battle, and no one's better at it than you."

I felt my heart rate spike. "Uh, that sounds like a lot of responsibility for someone who just learned about their magical stats like, five minutes ago."

"You're a natural," he said, like that explained everything.

"A natural at... what exactly?" I asked. "Magic? Leading armies? Saving the world?"

The second angel jumped in, unhelpfully. "All of the above."

"Perfect," I muttered. "Just perfect."

The first angel clapped again, clearly ignoring my rising panic. "Now, your companions will be arriving soon. The leaders of the other factions will need to meet with you."

Companions? Oh no. No way. "Let me guess," I said, rubbing my temples. "There are more 'chosen ones'?"

"Exactly," the angel said cheerfully. "You'll need to coordinate with them. Delver, leader of the Phoenix faction. Akuma, leader of Avian. And Atticus, leader of the Hell faction."

Atticus. Of course. My best friend—and boyfriend—Atticus was now part of this cosmic mess, too. And not just any part—he was the second strongest being on Earth, right behind me.

My mind flashed back to the days when we'd bicker over who would win in a video game, or who got to pick the movie. Little did I know we'd end up in a life-or-death race to save the planet from aliens. Romantic, right?

"Are you telling me that Atticus is now in charge of something called the Hell faction?" I asked, trying not to laugh at the absurdity of it all.

The angel looked at me seriously, not a trace of humor in his face. "Yes, Hell is one of the most formidable magical factions, known for summoning and controlling fire. He's a perfect fit."

Atticus would probably love that. Fire powers? Being in charge of something called Hell? Yeah, that sounded right up his alley. I imagined him smirking, probably thrilled with his cool new title.

"Great," I said. "So, what's the plan? Do we just... go to war?"

The angel nodded. "Sort of. You've got 1,000 years to prepare. During this time, all burdens of the world—disease, hunger, aging—are lifted. You'll spend that time building, training, and evolving."

"Evolving? Like the thing with the glowing rock?"

"Exactly," the angel said. "Except not just you. The entire human race will have the chance to evolve—become stronger, faster, more powerful. You and the other faction leaders will guide them."

This was too much. I had only just woken up, and now I was suddenly a magical dragon commander, preparing to lead humanity into a war against aliens in 1,000 years? Why couldn't I have just gotten a normal Tuesday?

"Alright," I said, sighing, "when do we start?"

"Right now, actually," the angel said brightly. "The first thing we need to do is get you to the Dragon faction headquarters. It's... well, let's just say it's a bit of a fixer-upper."

"Wait, we have a headquarters?"

"Of course! It's, uh... under construction. You'll get to oversee the building process. The angels are helping with that, but you'll need to guide them."

I groaned. "This just keeps getting better."

Before I could fully process the next step of my cosmic promotion, I heard a familiar voice behind me.

"Well, if it isn't our fearless leader!"

I turned around to see none other than Atticus himself, walking toward me with that signature grin plastered on his face. His eyes lit up with a mischievous gleam, and I had to admit, he looked... annoyingly good for someone who had probably just woken up to a similar life-altering alarm.

"Atticus," I said, rolling my eyes. "Let me guess—you're loving this."

He smirked. "Oh, I've been waiting for a promotion to 'Lord of Hell' my whole life."

Typical.

So there we were. Me, newly crowned leader of the Dragon faction, and Atticus, Lord of Hell (because of course he was). Next up, we'd meet the other two faction leaders and start building an army, all while figuring out how to train humans for a war with aliens. No big deal, right?

Just another normal day on Earth.

CHAPTER TWO

Apparently, I Run a Dragon Army Now

If you've ever wanted to know what it feels like to go from "regular person" to "supreme commander of an entire magical army," the answer is: exhausting. Like, way more exhausting than it should be, considering I didn't even do anything yet. One second, I'm Eleanor, living a pretty normal life, and the next, I'm supposed to lead a bunch of dragon-powered warriors into battle. Against aliens. Because apparently, that's my thing now.

And the best part? My faction headquarters—Dragon HQ, as I decided to call it—was, to put it politely, a mess.

We arrived there about an hour after my "evolution," flying across the sky courtesy of the angel brigade. And let me tell you, it wasn't the grand, fire-breathing castle I'd imagined. Nope. The place looked like someone had forgotten it even existed for a few hundred years. Crumbling walls, overgrown plants, and what I think was a dragon nest off in the corner. Cozy.

"So... this is it?" I asked, staring at what looked like the remains of a medieval fortress mixed with a haunted house.

One of the angels nodded enthusiastically. "Yep! Welcome to Dragon HQ. This will be the heart of your operations for the next 1,000 years. We've got big plans to spruce it up, though."

"Spruce it up?" I echoed, raising an eyebrow. "Is that angel talk for 'bulldoze it and start over?'"

He chuckled. "Don't worry, Eleanor. It may not look like much now, but with your leadership, it'll become the most powerful magical stronghold in the world."

"No pressure," I muttered, trying to wrap my head around the fact that I was supposed to turn this place into a fortress worthy of battling aliens.

Atticus, of course, found this all highly amusing. “Looks like you’ve got your work cut out for you, Dragon Queen,” he said with a smirk, casually leaning against a broken stone wall like he wasn’t in the middle of a post-apocalyptic fixer-upper. “Need a hand? Or maybe a flamethrower?”

I shot him a look. “Don’t you have a Hell HQ to set on fire?”

He shrugged. “We’ll see how it goes. Fire’s always a good start.”

That’s when I heard a loud crack behind me. I whipped around to see Delver—the leader of the Phoenix faction—appear in a blaze of light, landing with all the grace of a superhero in an action movie. His fiery red hair practically screamed Phoenix, and his eyes flashed like he was ready to explode into action at any moment.

Delver didn’t waste time. He strode toward me, arms crossed, looking me up and down like he was sizing up his competition. “Eleanor, right? Heard you’re the Dragon leader.”

I nodded, a little taken aback by his intensity. “Yeah, that’s me. You must be Delver.”

“Correct,” he said, eyes narrowing. “You better be ready. We don’t have time to mess around. The Phoenix faction doesn’t play games.”

Atticus snorted. “Wow, is that your official slogan? ‘We don’t play games’? Riveting stuff, Delver.”

Delver ignored him. “Our factions will need to work together to make sure humanity stands a chance. Phoenix and Dragon—both magical, both front-liners. We’ll be responsible for taking the fight to the aliens.”

I raised an eyebrow. “And you just assume we’ll be getting along?”

He smirked. “You tell me, Dragon Queen.”

Ugh. Another nickname. Great.

Before I could respond, a sharp whistle echoed through the sky. A large shadow swooped down, and Akuma, leader of the Avian faction, landed gracefully beside us. She was tall, elegant, and had an aura of someone who’d seen way too much in too little time. Her jet-black wings folded behind her, and her piercing gaze surveyed us with quiet authority.

“Are we really starting the ‘who’s got the coolest faction’ contest already?” she asked dryly, brushing her dark hair out of her face. “Because if we are, I should mention that my Avian warriors don’t even need magic to tear through an army.”

Atticus raised a hand. “I’d like to second that, actually. Hell is a strictly magical faction, but we’ve got some, uh, spicy tactics up our sleeves.”

Akuma rolled her eyes. “Of course you do.”

Delver, unfazed by the banter, looked between me and Akuma. "So, the physical factions—yours and Serpent—are going to handle gathering intel, right? You'll be the ones working in the shadows, striking where the enemy least expects it."

Akuma nodded. "Exactly. My Avians will specialize in scouting, infiltration, and aerial assaults. We're the ones who'll get the intel to give you all an edge. Serpent, too, but they're more on the sneaky side of things."

She cast a glance at the Serpent HQ in the distance—shrouded in mist and mystery, like they were already hiding in the shadows. Perfect for them, I thought.

I folded my arms, trying to process everything. "Alright, so we've got four factions, and each has its own strengths. We'll need to coordinate, train, and, I guess, build... all this. We've got 1,000 years, but something tells me it's not going to feel like that long."

Delver nodded. "Exactly. Phoenix and Dragon are front-line fighters, and we'll handle the brunt of the combat when the time comes. Avian and Serpent will gather intel, take care of recon, and handle special ops. Hell..." he trailed off, glancing at Atticus.

Atticus flashed a grin. "Hell burns everything to the ground."

I shot him a look. "You're going to have to be a little more strategic than that."

He shrugged, still smirking. "Details, details."

I sighed. This was my team. Magical warriors, aerial scouts, stealthy assassins, and a guy whose entire battle plan revolved around setting things on fire. And somehow, I was the one in charge of keeping them all together.

No big deal.

By the end of the day, we had a loose plan: fix up the headquarters, start training, and figure out how to harness our powers as faction leaders. We had angels helping us with resources and building, but the bulk of the responsibility fell on us.

I found myself standing at the edge of the cliff near the Dragon HQ, watching the horizon as the sun set. The weight of everything was finally hitting me. This was real. I was the last Greatest Dragon. I had to lead an army. And in 1,000 years, we'd be fighting to save humanity from aliens that were way beyond anything we'd ever faced.

Atticus appeared beside me, quiet for once. He didn't say anything, but I could feel his presence—steady, reassuring, even if he was probably thinking about fireballs.

"Hey," he said finally, "you okay?"

I glanced at him, then back at the sunset. "Yeah, I'm just... wrapping my head around all this."

He chuckled softly. "Yeah, me too. But hey, if anyone can do it, it's you. You're the Dragon Queen, after all."

I rolled my eyes. "Please stop calling me that."

"Never."

We stood there in silence for a while, watching the sky turn from orange to deep purple. The future felt uncertain, but for the first time that day, I felt a little more grounded. Atticus was right—if anyone could handle this crazy new world, it was me.

Because, whether I liked it or not, I was the leader of the Dragon faction now.

And I wasn't going to let anyone down.

I glanced around the crumbling courtyard, taking in the scattered debris and the hints of potential. "Look, I appreciate the enthusiasm for fire, Atticus, but we need a plan. We can't just wing it."

Delver crossed his arms, smirking. "And here I thought you'd embrace the chaotic side of battle."

"Chaos isn't a strategy," I shot back, straightening up. "We need to figure out our strengths and weaknesses. We should hold training sessions for everyone, not just the front-liners."

Akuma nodded, her expression serious. "Exactly. We can't rely solely on our powers. We need tactics. Strategies. And teamwork. Otherwise, we might as well throw ourselves into a dragon's mouth."

"Which, by the way, I wouldn't mind doing, if it meant getting out of this paperwork," Atticus joked, gesturing to the stacks of scrolls and charts that the angels had left for us. "What is all this? A guide to dragon etiquette?"

"Actually, it's a roster of potential recruits for each faction, along with their percentages," I explained, trying to sound more knowledgeable than I felt. "We need to assess our resources if we want to build a solid army."

As I sifted through the scrolls, I spotted names and numbers that made my head spin. Every human on the planet had received their percentage and classification, and now we had to figure out how to gather the best warriors from each faction. "We should hold a meeting with everyone to explain our plans and get everyone on board."

Delver smirked again. "So you're planning to be the big, bad Dragon Queen, huh?"

"Let's not go overboard," I replied, rolling my eyes. "I'm just trying to be a leader. And part of being a leader is keeping everyone informed."

Akuma glanced at Delver. "You know, I think Eleanor might be onto something. We can't afford to have anyone left in the dark. We need to unite our factions if we're going to survive this."

Atticus pretended to think hard. "And if it all goes wrong? Can I still light things on fire?"

"Maybe save that for the practice sessions?" I suggested, suppressing a laugh. "Alright, let's gather everyone. The sooner we get started, the better."

About an hour later...

The courtyard buzzed with nervous energy as warriors from all factions gathered. I stood at the center, trying to project an air of confidence, but inside, I felt like a kid playing dress-up. Atticus, Delver, and Akuma stood beside me, their expressions ranging from excitement to mild skepticism.

"Okay, everyone!" I called out, my voice carrying through the crowd. "Welcome to the first official meeting of the Dragon faction! I know things have been a little chaotic since the whole 'aliens are coming' situation, but we need to get serious. I'm Eleanor, your leader, and together, we're going to build the strongest army humanity has ever seen!"

A smattering of applause followed, but it was half-hearted, likely because everyone was still reeling from the shocking change in their lives.

"First," I continued, "let's talk about our strengths. The Dragon faction is magical and powerful, but we can't win this alone. We need to work closely with the Phoenix, Avian, and Serpent factions. Each of you has a role to play."

I paused, scanning the crowd. Some looked eager; others appeared skeptical. "Delver, would you like to introduce yourself?"

Delver stepped forward, his fiery hair catching the sunlight. "I'm Delver, leader of the Phoenix faction. We're all about explosive attacks and aerial assaults. Think of us as the high-flying shock troops. If you need someone to dive in and rain fire from above, we're your guys."

A few cheers erupted, and I noticed some warriors exchange excited glances.

"Next up, Akuma!" I gestured toward her.

She stepped forward, her wings unfurling dramatically. "I'm Akuma, leader of the Avian faction. We specialize in scouting and intelligence gathering. We're the ones who'll be flying above the battlefield, giving you the intel you need to strike. Without our eyes in the sky, you could be walking into a trap."

I could see the nods of agreement from the crowd. Good. Everyone needed to know we were a team.

"And last but not least, the charming Atticus," I said, shooting him a teasing smile.

Atticus stepped forward, casually leaning on a nearby wall. "Hey, I'm Atticus, leader of the Hell faction. We may not be the most traditional bunch, but we bring the heat. Literally. We'll handle the brute force and tactical flair—think of us as the wild card in your deck."

He flashed a grin that drew laughter from the crowd. I could tell he was winning them over.

"Alright," I said, taking a deep breath. "We'll be establishing training sessions, and we need volunteers for each faction to help with planning and strategizing. Remember, this is a fight for our future. If we want to survive this war, we need to unite and prepare together."

As the meeting progressed, I started to feel a sense of purpose. People were willing to step up, to fight for our survival. The worries and fears I'd had began to melt away, replaced by determination. We were in this together.

At the end of the meeting, as everyone dispersed, I found myself alone for a moment. Delver and Akuma were deep in conversation, while Atticus wandered off to poke at some of the newly installed dragon decorations—don't ask.

Just then, I noticed a figure lingering at the edge of the courtyard. It was a young girl, no older than fifteen, looking a bit lost. Her vibrational percentage was glowing orange, signaling that she was physical. She was dressed in torn jeans and a faded t-shirt, her brown hair falling into her eyes.

I walked over, kneeling down to her level. "Hey there! What's your name?"

She looked up, wide-eyed. "Uh, I'm Cora. I just got my percentage, and I—um, I want to help. But I don't know how."

I smiled gently. "Cora, every single person has something to offer. We need fighters, builders, strategists—everyone plays a role. If you want to help, we'll find a place for you. How do you feel about training?"

Her eyes lit up. "I'd love that! I can fight. I've been practicing since I was little!"

"Perfect!" I said, standing up. "Join us for the next training session. You'll fit right in."

As she nodded, I couldn't shake the feeling that this girl, along with many others, would play a pivotal role in our fight against the aliens. We were building a community, a family, forged by fire and determination.

And as the sun dipped below the horizon, casting long shadows over Dragon HQ, I felt a flicker of hope spark within me.

Maybe we really could do this.

CHAPTER THREE

Training Day: Fire and Flight

The morning sun peeked through the clouds, casting a warm glow over Dragon HQ. I rubbed the sleep from my eyes, the adrenaline from yesterday's meeting still buzzing in my veins. Today was the day we started our training, and I could feel the weight of responsibility pressing down on me like a dragon's tail.

After a quick breakfast—which consisted of questionable angelic pastries—I gathered my fellow leaders for a final pep talk before the chaos began. Atticus was lounging against a wall, tossing a fireball between his hands like it was a mere plaything. Delver was practicing his aerial maneuvers with a few of the Phoenix recruits, his flames trailing behind him in brilliant streaks. Akuma was deep in conversation with some Avian scouts, discussing their plans for aerial reconnaissance.

"Alright, everyone," I said, clapping my hands to grab their attention. "Today marks the beginning of our training. I want to see everyone at their best. Remember, we need to unite our factions and develop strategies that will work for each of us."

Atticus smirked, his trademark charm lighting up the area. "You mean 'strategies that involve setting things on fire,' right?"

I rolled my eyes, fighting back a grin. "Maybe let's save the fire for the battlefield, shall we? We need to focus on teamwork."

Akuma chimed in, her wings fluttering excitedly. "I can't wait to see how the Avian scouts work with the Dragons. Imagine the aerial attacks we could pull off!"

Delver swooped down, a playful grin plastered on his face. "Just remember, if we're practicing air support, no crashing into each other. I've had enough of 'fireball dodgeball' for one day."

With a few chuckles exchanged, we headed out to the training grounds. As I stepped into the open area, I was greeted by a cacophony of activity.

Recruits from all factions were already warming up, stretching their limbs, and chatting excitedly. I spotted Cora among them, her face flushed with enthusiasm as she chatted with a couple of older Dragon recruits.

"Cora!" I called, waving her over. "How are you feeling?"

She beamed at me, her brown hair bouncing as she jogged over. "I can't believe I'm finally training with everyone! I've been waiting for this!"

"Great! Let's start with some basics," I said, leading her toward a group of recruits. "You'll want to keep your stance low and your focus sharp. Remember, training is as much about mindset as it is about strength."

As I led the group through warm-ups, Atticus demonstrated a few fiery moves that left everyone in awe. With a flick of his wrist, he conjured a flaming sword, the flames dancing dangerously close but somehow never burning anything. "Alright, who wants to give it a try?"

Several recruits stepped up, eager to impress. The air crackled with excitement as flames flickered to life in their hands, some more successful than others. Cora was one of the last to step up, her face set in determination. I watched with bated breath as she summoned her own small fireball, a flicker of orange illuminating her face.

"Not bad, Cora!" I cheered, encouraging her.

"Thanks! I've been practicing!" she replied, grinning from ear to ear.

As we moved on to more serious drills, I decided to put everyone through a series of obstacle courses designed to test their agility, strength, and teamwork. It was a chaotic mix of dodging fireballs, scaling walls, and flying through hoops. I observed as groups of Dragons and Phoenixes worked together, some struggling while others soared through the challenges.

"Focus on communication!" I shouted over the din. "If you don't work together, you'll trip over each other."

The first few attempts were rough, with recruits getting tangled in ropes or missing their targets entirely. But slowly, they began to adapt, finding their rhythm as they cheered each other on. I could feel my heart swell with pride. This was what we needed—unity in the face of adversity.

By midday, the sun was blazing overhead, and the heat was starting to get to us. I called a break, letting everyone grab water and catch their breath. As I leaned against a wall, I noticed Delver chatting animatedly with some of the Phoenix recruits, demonstrating a few acrobatic flips. His laughter echoed through the courtyard, drawing a crowd.

"Hey, Eleanor!" he shouted, catching my eye. "Why don't you join us? Show them what the Dragon Queen can do!"

I raised an eyebrow. "Are you challenging me to a flying contest?"

"Why not?" He spread his arms wide. "Let's see who's got the better moves!"

The crowd roared with excitement, and I felt a thrill of adrenaline course through me. Why not? After all, if I was going to lead these people, I needed to show them I was capable of more than just strategy.

"Alright, you're on!" I called back, flashing a competitive grin.

We took to the air, and the rush of wind against my face was exhilarating. I spread my wings, reveling in the newfound freedom. Delver darted ahead, executing flips and rolls with a grace that made me momentarily jealous. I focused on keeping up, weaving through the air and mimicking his movements.

"Not bad!" Delver called out, his voice laced with laughter. "But can you do this?"

With a flick of his wrist, he ignited his wings in flames, leaving a trail of fiery sparkles behind him as he dove toward the ground. My jaw dropped in disbelief.

"Show off!" I laughed, but a spark of inspiration ignited within me. I hadn't tried combining my magic with my flight yet.

Determined, I took a deep breath and focused. I summoned the fire within me, letting it envelop my wings. With a burst of energy, I dove after him, leaving a trail of flame in my wake.

The crowd erupted in cheers, and I could hear the excitement in their voices as we performed our aerial dance. It felt incredible, and for a moment, all my worries faded away. This was what it meant to be a Dragon—to fight, to soar, and to inspire.

After our impromptu aerial display, we landed back in the courtyard, both breathless and grinning. I could see the spark of motivation ignited in the other recruits' eyes, and I felt a wave of pride wash over me. We were building something special—a community that would fight for each other, no matter what.

As the day wore on, the training continued. I was surprised by how quickly everyone was adapting, but I knew that this was just the beginning. We had a long road ahead, and the aliens were still lurking in the shadows.

That evening, as the sun dipped below the horizon, casting the sky in hues of orange and pink, we gathered around a fire pit for a debrief. The mood was lighter than earlier, with laughter echoing through the air as we shared stories of our training mishaps.

"Remember when Delver tried to impress us with that backflip and landed straight in a bush?" Atticus teased, pointing at Delver, who blushed a deep crimson.

"I was trying to show off!" Delver retorted, but the laughter only grew louder.

As the sun set and the stars began to twinkle above us, I couldn't help but feel a sense of hope. We might not be prepared for the battle that lay ahead, but we were building a team. A family. And together, we were stronger.

Tomorrow would bring new challenges, but for tonight, we could revel in the victory of simply coming together.

And as I watched my friends laughing and sharing stories, I realized one thing: we were ready to face whatever came our way.

As the laughter died down, I leaned back in my seat, allowing the crackling fire to warm my skin. It felt good to let loose, even if it was just for a little while. But of course, my moment of bliss was about to be shattered.

"So, Eleanor," Atticus said, a mischievous glint in his eye. "What's the plan for the Dragon faction's official training motto?"

I raised an eyebrow, sensing trouble. "What do you mean?"

"Every good faction needs a motto! Something inspiring! Something that'll make our enemies quiver in their boots! Something like... 'Dragons: We're Hotter Than You!'" He struck a dramatic pose, holding his flaming sword aloft like some sort of ridiculous hero.

The recruits burst into laughter, but I couldn't help but groan. "Seriously? That's your idea of an inspirational battle cry?"

"Hey, it has a nice ring to it!" he defended, fanning his flames. "Plus, who wouldn't be intimidated by a faction with a motto about being literally on fire?"

Delver piped up, chuckling. "We could always go for 'Dragons: Scorching Your Problems Since Time Immemorial.'"

"Or how about 'Dragons: We Burn Down the Competition—Literally'?" Akuma added with a wink, clearly enjoying the banter.

I held my head in my hands, trying to suppress a grin. "Okay, okay! Let's dial it down a bit before we give the aliens an aneurysm with our puns."

Suddenly, a distant clang echoed through the training grounds, drawing our attention. I turned to see a couple of Serpent recruits tangled up in a mess of ropes. One of them was attempting to perform some sort of stealth maneuver while the other had somehow ended up upside down in a bush, looking thoroughly confused.

"Ah, the infamous training tactic known as 'The Great Ropes of Doom,'" I joked, trying to hold back my laughter. "I hear it's a fan favorite among the Serpent recruits."

"Let's be real," Delver said, suppressing his own laughter. "They should probably stick to stealth training. That bush is way too big for them."

With that, we all burst into laughter again, our spirits soaring. Just then, an angelic figure landed nearby, her golden hair shimmering like it was straight out of a shampoo commercial. I had to suppress the urge to squint against the blinding glow.

"Hey! What's so funny?" she asked, hands on her hips, looking like she just walked off a celestial catwalk.

"Just a little friendly banter," I said, gesturing toward the tangled recruits. "You know, keeping morale up while we prepare for the alien apocalypse."

"Sounds like fun! Just make sure you're also preparing for the actual war," she replied, her tone shifting to something more serious. "You can't rely on humor alone, you know. The aliens won't find your jokes funny when they're blasting your cities to ashes."

I nodded, feeling the weight of her words settle on my shoulders. "Right, of course. Just trying to keep things light before we all turn into intense battle machines."

She raised an eyebrow. "You sure you're ready for this?"

I took a deep breath. "Well, I'm the greatest dragon since the days of yore, or whatever they say. I think I can handle a few aliens, right?"

"Sure, if you don't mind being roasted," she replied with a smirk before taking off again, her wings leaving a trail of golden sparkles.

As night fell, we wrapped up our training session and gathered around the fire once more. The stars twinkled above, creating a cosmic backdrop for our shenanigans. I decided it was time to lighten the mood again, so I clapped my hands together and stood up.

"Alright, everyone! Time for the real bonding exercise! We're going to share our most embarrassing training moments! I'll go first!"

"What? No! You can't just make this a thing!" Akuma protested, though I could see the glimmer of curiosity in her eyes.

"Too late! I'll start! So, during my first training session, I was supposed to summon a tiny fireball, right? Well, I was so nervous that I accidentally conjured a massive firestorm instead! You should've seen the look on

Atticus's face as he dove for cover. It was like watching a flaming ostrich try to escape a lion."

"Hey! I thought the world was ending!" Atticus retorted, hands raised defensively.

"Yeah, but you were flapping your arms like they were wings! It was a beautiful sight," I teased, and the recruits howled with laughter.

"I'm sure it was," Delver chimed in, "but nothing compares to the time I accidentally got stuck in a tree while trying to impress some recruits with my aerial skills. I ended up looking like a bird caught in a windstorm!"

"Better than the time I slipped off a training pole and fell into the nearest barrel of water," Akuma said, shaking her head. "Let's just say, I got really familiar with the fish population in the training grounds."

The stories continued to flow, each one more absurd than the last. Soon, everyone was laughing so hard that their sides hurt. The night was alive with camaraderie and banter, the bonds between us growing stronger as we shared our ridiculous experiences.

As I watched my friends laugh and reminisce, I couldn't shake the feeling that we were exactly what this world needed. We were more than just warriors; we were a family forged in fire, laughter, and the promise of something greater.

Just then, the sky above us darkened, and a soft rumble rolled through the air. "Uh, guys?" I said, looking up. "That doesn't look like a good sign."

Delver squinted, his playful grin fading. "Is it just me, or does it feel like something's about to come crashing down?"

Before anyone could respond, a brilliant flash of light illuminated the night sky, and the ground shook beneath us. It was like the universe itself was trying to tell us something.

"Okay, definitely not a good sign," I muttered, my heart racing.

The laughter died down, replaced by a tense silence. We all exchanged worried glances, the weight of our upcoming battle hanging in the air like a storm cloud. But one thing was clear—we were ready to face whatever challenges awaited us.

Because we were the Dragons, and we burned bright, ready to light up the darkness.

CHAPTER FOUR

A Crash Course in Faction Drama

The moment the blinding light faded and the ground settled, we exchanged looks that could've been mistaken for a mix of awe and sheer panic. "Well, that was a fun distraction," I said, trying to sound nonchalant while my heart raced like a caffeinated squirrel. "Anyone want to guess what that was?"

"Probably the aliens trying to make their grand entrance," Akuma said, folding her arms. "You know, to remind us we're supposed to be preparing for their apocalypse, not our own comedic drama."

"Yeah, right," I said, rolling my eyes. "They probably heard we were having a bonding moment and got jealous. Not everyone can have such stunning hair and humor like us."

"Speaking of which, my hair is still wet from that barrel incident!" Akuma shot back, but I could see a grin creeping onto her face. "But hey, I'll take looking fabulous over being fried by aliens any day!"

"Can't argue with that logic," Delver chimed in, giving her a thumbs-up. "Just remember: if we get vaporized, we'll never get to see how we look in those post-war family portraits."

"Right? I'd hate for my legacy to be a messy hairdo and a sunburn," I added, and with that, we all burst into laughter again, the tension momentarily forgotten.

But then, the training ground erupted into chaos. An alarm blared overhead, its shrill wail cutting through our laughter like a knife through butter. "Oh great," Atticus said, eyes wide. "Now what?"

A booming voice echoed over the loudspeakers: "ATTENTION ALL RECRUITS! REPORT TO THE CENTRAL COMMAND AT ONCE! IMMINENT DANGER APPROACHING!"

"Well, that sounds delightful," I said, sarcasm dripping from my words. "I was hoping for a relaxing evening of tea and not-so-great jokes. But alas, duty calls."

"Let's move before they decide we're too busy having fun to notice the end of the world," Delver said, already sprinting toward the command center, his wings trailing behind him like a proud peacock.

We all followed, sprinting through the training grounds, hearts pounding with excitement—and maybe a hint of dread. Arriving at the command center felt like stepping into a sci-fi movie, complete with flashing screens and angels barking orders like drill sergeants.

"Where's the fire?!" I called out, half-joking, half-serious.

"Don't worry, we're not on fire—yet," one of the angels replied, her expression deadpan. "But the aliens have sent a massive wave of drones our way, and we need to prepare for immediate combat."

"Drones?" Atticus asked, brow furrowed. "Do they at least come with snacks?"

I facepalmed, while the angel just rolled her eyes. "No, but I assure you, they'll be far more dangerous than a vending machine malfunctioning."

"Not the vending machine!" Akuma gasped, clutching her heart dramatically. "I don't think I can handle the emotional trauma of losing my favorite snacks!"

"Focus, team!" I said, trying to maintain order. "What's the plan here?"

"Each faction will be assigned specific roles," the angel explained. "Dragons will focus on aerial attacks, Phoenixes will assist from the skies with explosive magic, and Serpents will handle reconnaissance. Griffins... well, they'll charge in headfirst and hope for the best."

"Sounds about right for the Griffins," I muttered. "Is that all we have? Just hope and a prayer?"

"Pretty much," the angel replied, her tone eerily calm. "But seriously, we're working on a strategy right now. We need everyone in their respective factions to prepare."

Before I could respond, the command center erupted with activity. Angels flew back and forth, issuing commands and adjusting the holographic displays of our impending doom. It was like watching a chaotic ballet where no one knew the choreography, and everyone was trying to avoid stepping on someone else's toes.

"Let's split up and get our squads ready," I said, taking charge. "Dragons, gather around! We need to make sure our firepower is ready to go. And for the love of everything holy, please don't blow anything up until we know what we're up against."

As the recruits gathered, I took a deep breath. "Alright, listen up! I know we've been having a good laugh, but it's time to get serious. The aliens are coming, and we're not just fighting for ourselves anymore; we're fighting for everyone on this planet."

"Does that mean we can still tell jokes?" Delver piped up, a hopeful look in his eyes.

"Only if they're good," I replied, crossing my arms. "I'm talking about quality material here, people. No more of Atticus's 'flaming' puns, or I'll personally throw you into the nearest bush."

"Hey! My jokes are top-notch!" Atticus protested, but the corners of his mouth were betraying him, twitching upward in a smirk.

"Let's get to it!" I called, trying to rein in the laughter. "The fate of the world is at stake! And if we're going down, we're going down in style—preferably with fewer awkward moments involving me falling out of trees."

The recruits cheered, rallying together as we prepared for what lay ahead. As we organized ourselves and shared last-minute strategies, the weight of our mission settled on my shoulders. But even amidst the chaos, I felt a flicker of hope.

As the chaos continued to whirl around us, I could feel the excitement buzzing in the air like a swarm of caffeinated bees. The recruits were rallying together, adrenaline pumping as they strapped on their gear and gathered their weapons. It was a scene reminiscent of an epic battle montage from one of those blockbuster films—minus the dramatic music and the slow-motion running.

"Alright, Dragons, let's check our gear!" I called out, attempting to sound authoritative while secretly hoping I wouldn't trip over my own feet. "Flaming swords? Check! Fireproof armor? Check! Sassy comebacks ready to go?"

"Always!" Atticus chimed in, raising his sword like a knight about to slay a dragon—ironic, considering we were supposed to be the dragons.

As I surveyed our little group, I noticed Delver fiddling with something shiny in his hands. "What's that?" I asked, tilting my head curiously.

"This?" he said, holding up what looked like a small, ornate dagger. "I figured we might need a backup plan, you know, just in case our firepower needs a little... finesse."

"Are you saying our firepower is too loud?" Akuma teased, elbowing him playfully. "Please, we're not a marching band! We're dragons! Loud and proud!"

"Just remember, a well-placed strike can be more effective than a flaming inferno," Delver shot back with a wink.

"Hey, I'm all for finesse, but let's not forget our roots," I said, crossing my arms. "We are dragons, after all. We should be roaring, not sneaking around like a bunch of overgrown mice!"

"Overgrown mice?" Akuma snorted. "Now that's an image I can't unsee! Can you imagine a bunch of giant mice with wings and fire breath?"

I burst out laughing at the mental picture. "Honestly, I'd be more worried about cheese supplies than the aliens!"

The banter continued as we double-checked our gear. With each laugh and every ridiculous comment, the weight of the situation seemed to lighten.

Just as we were about to head out, a booming voice echoed through the command center again. "DRAGONS, REPORT TO YOUR POSITIONS IMMEDIATELY!"

"That sounded urgent," I muttered, feeling a pang of nervousness in my gut. "Time to put on our brave faces, folks! And remember, if you're feeling scared, just imagine the aliens trying to run with those weird tentacle legs they have!"

We filed out of the command center and headed towards our designated positions. The night air was thick with tension, and the stars above seemed to twinkle in anticipation. As we reached the edge of the training grounds, I could see the faint outline of the alien drones hovering in the distance, their metallic bodies glinting ominously in the moonlight.

"Wow, they really know how to make an entrance, don't they?" Delver muttered, peering into the darkness. "I mean, look at that! It's like they took 'dramatic reveal' lessons from a Hollywood director!"

"Just wait until they start their monologue," I replied, squinting at the approaching figures. "I hear they have a real knack for long-winded speeches about 'galactic domination' and 'the futility of resistance.'"

"Don't forget the part where they say we're insignificant," Akuma added with a grin. "They really know how to make us feel special, don't they?"

As the drones drew closer, my heart raced. I could feel the heat of my fire building within me, ready to erupt at a moment's notice. "Alright, Dragons! Let's show these tin cans what we're made of! On my signal, we unleash our fiery fury!"

"Are we sure about this?" Delver asked, his usual bravado wavering slightly. "What if they're actually here to, I don't know, ask us for directions?"

"Directions to where?" I countered, raising an eyebrow. "The nearest black hole? The 'Doomed Planet' gift shop?"

Just then, the first drone zipped overhead, and I could see a beam of light cutting through the darkness. "Uh-oh, they've spotted us!" I shouted. "Time to put our fire-breathing skills to the test!"

With a battle cry that echoed across the training grounds, I unleashed a torrent of flames, sending them soaring toward the oncoming drones. The fire blazed bright, illuminating the night and revealing the swarm of mechanical foes heading our way.

"Now that's what I'm talking about!" Atticus shouted, igniting his sword with fiery passion. "Let's turn up the heat!"

As the flames met the drones, a series of explosions erupted in the air, sending sparks flying like confetti at a celebration. The drones started to veer off course, their once-menacing presence now flickering with uncertainty.

"Ha! Take that!" I yelled, feeling a surge of confidence. "Who's the overgrown mouse now?"

"More like an overgrown dragon with a serious flare for the dramatic!" Delver added, a grin spreading across his face.

But just as we were reveling in our fiery victory, the remaining drones shifted their formation, and I noticed something even more alarming. "Uh, guys? I think they're regrouping!"

"Great, because nothing says 'we're in trouble' quite like an enemy regrouping," Akuma said, her voice dripping with sarcasm. "What's next? A motivational speech?"

I took a deep breath, grounding myself in the moment. "Alright, Dragons! We need to regroup and strategize! Time to channel our inner dragon and take charge!"

As we huddled together, adrenaline coursing through our veins, I felt a sense of unity that ignited my heart. We were more than just a faction; we were a family ready to take on the universe—one fireball and laugh at a time.

"On three! One, two, three—Dragons!" I roared, our voices echoing as we prepared for the next wave.

"Let's give these aliens a welcome they'll never forget!" Atticus added, and we charged forward, ready to face whatever chaos awaited us.

CHAPTER FIVE

The Calm Before the Tech Storm

The smoke from our fiery defense hung in the air, swirling like an ominous fog as we gathered ourselves after the initial onslaught. The drones had fizzled out, their circuits fried like a bad egg left on the stove too long. In the aftermath, the training ground resembled a battlefield, with scorched earth and bits of machinery strewn about like confetti at a failed parade.

“Great job, everyone!” I shouted, trying to rally the troops. “If there’s one thing we’ve learned today, it’s that we make excellent toast!”

“Yeah, toast with a side of chaos,” Akuma replied, brushing ash from her shoulders. “Next time, maybe we can avoid the whole ‘fiery explosions’ thing? My hair doesn’t handle that well.”

“Your hair looks fabulous, even in ashes,” I assured her, and she smiled, tossing her hair over her shoulder dramatically.

Delver was examining the remains of one of the drones, his brow furrowed in concentration. “These aren’t just regular drones,” he murmured, picking up a singed piece of metal. “They have some advanced tech embedded in them. I mean, look at this circuitry!”

“Congratulations, Delver! You’ve discovered the concept of technology!” Atticus quipped, leaning in to inspect the charred remains. “What’s next? Are you going to invent a new game called ‘Spot the Drone?’”

Delver shot him a mock glare. “Very funny. I’m just saying we should analyze these. We might find something useful for the real aliens when they show up.”

“Or at least a decent recipe for disaster,” I added, trying to keep the mood light. “But you’re right. Let’s gather what we can. I can already hear the angel’s voice in my head: ‘Research is key!’”

"Just what I want to hear before bed," Akuma sighed dramatically, but I could see she was still all in. "What if we come across alien cuisine? I don't think my stomach is ready for that kind of adventure."

As we picked through the wreckage, the laughter and banter eased the tension lingering in the air. Each charred drone piece was another reminder of our preparation for something bigger, something we couldn't yet comprehend.

Eventually, we gathered enough remains to make a decent pile. Delver laid out the findings on a nearby table in the command center, a look of determination on his face. "Alright, let's get to work. We need to figure out what makes these things tick."

"Shouldn't we call in the big guns?" I suggested, glancing around the bustling command center filled with angels barking orders and recruits scurrying like ants. "I mean, we're not exactly rocket scientists here."

"Speak for yourself," Delver replied, grinning. "I've seen a few documentaries. I'm basically an expert."

We gathered around the table, where Delver began pointing out the intricacies of the drone's design. "These components are designed for agility and speed. They can process information faster than any human could. If we're going to beat the aliens, we need to understand how to outsmart their technology."

"Outsmart technology? You mean like having a dance-off with a computer?" Akuma quipped. "I can see the headline now: 'Dragons Dance, Drones Dazed!'"

"Hey, it worked for us with the fire," I replied, feeling a surge of confidence. "We just need to channel our inner dragon and get creative."

Just then, an angel walked over, her expression serious. "What you've found is more valuable than you realize," she said, eyeing the drone parts. "But we need to move quickly. The next phase of our training is about to begin, and it's not going to be easy."

"Great! More fun! Just what I signed up for," I said, feigning enthusiasm. "What are we doing this time? Team-building exercises? Trust falls? I promise not to drop anyone... on purpose."

The angel sighed, but I could see a hint of amusement in her eyes. "This is serious. We need to prepare you for advanced combat scenarios. We'll be simulating battles, and you'll face the programmed drones in a controlled environment. This will help you develop tactics for when the real aliens come."

"Ah, nothing like a little simulated chaos to prepare us for actual chaos," Delver said, grinning. "Count me in!"

As we moved to the training arena, I couldn't help but feel a mixture of excitement and dread. The prospect of facing the drones again—this time with more realistic stakes—was daunting. But if we were going to take on an alien invasion, we had to embrace the chaos.

When we arrived, the arena was set up like an obstacle course, filled with barriers, targets, and everything short of an obstacle involving flaming hoops—which I was still pushing for. The drones hovered ominously at one end, their sensors flashing as they awaited activation.

"Alright, team!" I clapped my hands together, channeling all the pep talks I'd ever heard in school. "This is our chance to show those drones who's boss. We need to work together, strategize, and have some fun while doing it. Remember, every second counts!"

"Even the awkward ones?" Akuma asked, raising an eyebrow.

"Especially the awkward ones!" I replied with a grin. "Let's make sure the drones have a front-row seat to our ridiculousness!"

With that, the training exercise began. Drones shot through the air, zipping around with alarming speed, while we took our positions, trying our best to coordinate our attacks. It was like a chaotic dance party—except instead of music, we had the sounds of whirring machinery and the occasional shout of encouragement (or a cry of panic).

"Focus on teamwork!" I yelled, ducking as a drone whizzed past my head. "And remember: dragons don't dodge, we blaze!"

The first few rounds were a disaster, with drones zigzagging and buzzing around us like pesky flies. But slowly, we began to find our rhythm, our chaotic movements turning into a choreographed battle dance. Flames shot from our mouths, explosions erupted from the Phoenix faction, and the Griffins charged in, tackling drones with all the grace of... well, not much grace at all, but they sure knew how to make an entrance!

By the end of the training session, we were panting and covered in bits of drone debris, but we were grinning from ear to ear.

"Not bad for a first run," I said, wiping sweat from my brow. "If we can survive our own training, I'd say we're ready for whatever the universe throws at us."

"Let's just hope it's not another round of alien drone dance-offs," Delver added, laughter bubbling up among us.

As the sun began to set, casting a golden hue over our training grounds, I felt a sense of hope blossoming in my chest. We were becoming a team, one that could take on the universe—one ridiculous, fiery, and chaotic moment at a time.

And as we regrouped, exhausted but elated, I couldn't shake the feeling that we were just getting started.

The aliens might not be here yet, but we were ready to face anything—even if that meant facing our own ridiculousness head-on.

As the last drone clattered to the ground, Delver raised his arms in victory. "And that, my friends, is how you turn flying metal death machines into glorified paperweights!"

"Brilliant! Can we add that to the training manual?" Akuma joked, flicking a bit of drone ash off her shoulder. "Step one: make sure they know you're better at flying than they are."

Atticus laughed, wiping the sweat from his brow. "Great! Because my mom always said I should follow my dreams... unless those dreams involve being chased by robots!"

Just as we began to celebrate our hard-earned victory, the ground beneath us shook as if the universe itself had decided to applaud our brilliance (or was just having a caffeine-induced episode). I stumbled, grabbing onto the nearest thing—a rather unimpressed looking angel who was mid-conversation with another angel.

"Can you keep it down?" the angel huffed, adjusting her halo. "Some of us are trying to maintain a celestial level of professionalism here."

"Sorry, ma'am!" I said, feigning innocence. "We were just performing a highly skilled victory dance. You know, to celebrate our imminent domination over all mechanical life forms."

"Right," she replied, rolling her eyes. "I'm sure the aliens will be impressed by your 'dance moves.'"

"Hey, you never know!" Delver chimed in. "Next time we face off, we can do the 'Electric Slide' with the drones. They'll never see it coming!"

The angel looked like she was about to say something when suddenly the ground shook again, this time accompanied by a deep rumbling that sounded suspiciously like the universe clearing its throat—like a really big cosmic sneeze. It echoed through the training grounds, causing everyone to look around in alarm.

"What is that?" Akuma asked, eyes wide.

"I don't know, but if it's an alien attack, I'm totally blaming the drones!" I said, clenching my fists in an overly dramatic way. "We need to prepare ourselves! Brace for impact! Activate the 'Survive Alien Attack' plan!"

"What plan?" Atticus deadpanned, glancing around. "Is that the one where we just scream and hope for the best?"

"Exactly!" I grinned. "It's foolproof!"

Just then, a blinding light engulfed the training arena, casting eerie shadows on our faces, making us look like we were auditioning for the lead role in a horror film. Out of the light materialized a figure so dramatic that even the angels froze mid-angeling.

It was a larger-than-life angel, with shimmering wings that looked like they were made from stardust and a sword that sparkled like it had a personal vendetta against darkness. She landed with a thud that rattled the ground, and we all collectively held our breath.

"Fear not, brave warriors!" she proclaimed, her voice echoing as if she was narrating a really intense documentary. "I am Seraphina, the Guardian of the Realm!"

"Wait, the realm?" Akuma whispered, her eyes narrowing. "Are we in a video game now? Because I'm definitely not ready for another level!"

"Have you come to give us superpowers?" Delver asked, practically bouncing on his toes. "Or maybe a pizza? Because we've earned it after defeating those drones!"

Seraphina raised an eyebrow, her expression shifting to one of bemusement. "This is not a joke! The cosmos is in peril, and I come bearing news of grave importance!"

"Cosmic peril? Is it like a universal-sized hangover?" Atticus asked, trying to keep a straight face. "Because I've had one of those, and they're not pretty."

"No!" she snapped, her wings unfurling dramatically. "I mean real danger! The drones were merely a distraction, a test of your readiness. The true threat is far worse than you can imagine."

"Okay, but is it as bad as my last history exam?" I pressed, unable to resist the humor in the situation. "Because that was pretty apocalyptic."

"Focus!" Seraphina commanded, her tone fierce. "The forces of darkness are gathering, and they plan to strike soon. You must unite your factions, train harder than ever, and prepare for the battles to come!"

"Unite? Train harder?" I exclaimed, gesturing wildly. "I can barely convince these guys to eat their vegetables! You expect us to form an alliance like some superhero squad?"

"Indeed," she replied, her tone softening slightly. "Only together can you stand a chance against what is to come. The fate of Earth lies in your hands."

"So, basically, we're the chosen ones?" Akuma asked, glancing around as if expecting a shiny badge to appear. "Because I always thought we'd get a cooler title—like 'Guardians of Awesome' or something."

"Trust me, it's a lot less glamorous than it sounds," Seraphina said, her expression softening. "But it's true. You are pivotal to the survival of your kind."

"Okay, so what's the plan?" Delver asked, eyes gleaming with excitement. "More dance-offs? Because I'm totally in!"

"Enough with the dance-offs!" Seraphina exclaimed, her voice carrying authority. "You must use your skills wisely. Your training will evolve, and you'll face challenges that will test not just your powers, but your ability to work as a team."

"Sounds like a blast," I said, rolling my eyes. "I can't wait to see what kind of mind-bending puzzles you've got in store for us. Maybe a 'find the angel's halo' kind of game?"

"Just focus on your training," she reiterated, sounding like a cosmic mother trying to get her kids to clean their rooms. "The angels will assist you, but the final outcome rests on your shoulders. Prepare yourselves. You have much to learn."

And just like that, with a final sweep of her shimmering wings, Seraphina vanished back into the light, leaving us standing there, stunned, covered in drone debris, and a little unsure if we were actually the heroes of our own story or just the punchlines.

"Well, that was dramatic," I said, breaking the silence that followed. "What do you think? Superheroes in training or the universe's biggest joke?"

"I'm voting for both," Atticus replied with a grin. "I mean, if we can survive this training, we can survive anything. Even bad puns."

As we headed back to the command center, my mind raced with the possibilities ahead of us. I didn't know what Seraphina's cryptic warning meant, but one thing was for sure: if we were going to take on whatever darkness was looming out there, we'd have to do it together, in style—and maybe with a little more humor than usual.

"Alright, team," I said, determination igniting within me. "Let's get to work! We've got a universe to save, a reputation to uphold, and definitely some pizza to devour."

With that, we marched back into the fray, ready to embrace the absurdity of our quest. Because if there was one thing I knew for sure, it was that if we were going down, we were going down laughing.

CHAPTER SIX

New Base, Who Dis?

in time. Do not test me."

"Oh, we wouldn't dream of it," I said with an overly sweet smile. "But just curious, what exactly is this 'new base' going to do? Is it a fortress? A magical defense hub? Or, you know, just somewhere to store our collection of super powerful weapons?"

The angel's wings twitched as if they wanted to smack me upside the head. "It is your new strategic command post. A base of operations where you will train, strategize, and monitor the progress of the alien invasion."

"You had me at 'monitor,'" Akuma muttered. "Because nothing says 'heroic' like staring at a bunch of blinking lights all day."

"And who exactly is in charge of this 'strategic command post'?" I asked, already dreading the answer.

"You, Eleanor," the angel said with a straight face.

Oh no. Oh, no no no no no.

I barely trusted myself to make breakfast without setting the toaster on fire. And now I was supposed to manage an entire base? What was I supposed to do—hold meetings and assign tasks? "Hey, Atticus, can you file those reports on alien activity by the end of the day?" Yeah, right. I could barely get him to not light things on fire.

"Can I at least pick a cooler title?" I asked, desperate. "Like 'Supreme Commander' or 'Chief Badass of the Apocalypse'?"

"No," the angel said flatly.

Well, there went my dreams of having the coolest name in history.

Three hours later,

We stood in front of what we had managed to build so far. And let's just say... it wasn't looking great. Somehow, we'd constructed what could only be described as a "leaning tower of battle junk."

Atticus scratched his head, staring at the crooked walls. "I'm pretty sure buildings aren't supposed to do that."

"Do what?" Akuma asked.

"Lean like they're trying to moonwalk."

"It's fine," Delver said, ever the optimist. "If we just add a little more to the left, it'll straighten out. Probably. Maybe."

"Or it'll collapse in on itself and form a black hole," I sighed, rubbing my temples. "This is not how I envisioned saving the world. I figured we'd be doing more 'punch aliens in the face' and less 'build a wobbly fort in the woods.'"

At that moment, one of the lower walls gave an ominous creak, and before we could react, the entire thing came crashing down like a house of cards. Dust flew everywhere, and when the smoke cleared, we were left staring at a very large, very unstable pile of rubble.

"Well, that's just perfect," Akuma said dryly. "We've created the world's ugliest pile of scrap metal. Ten points to us."

"Hey, I blame the blueprint!" I threw my hands up defensively. "It was cursed from the start."

"You know what? Forget the building," Atticus groaned. "Let's just make a campfire, roast marshmallows, and hope the aliens are allergic to s'mores."

"I'm in," Delver said, already gathering sticks.

I wasn't sure how long we stood there, staring at the mess we had created, but it was clear we weren't going to win any architecture awards. If this was the base that was supposed to help us win the war, well... we were doomed.

But then something unexpected happened. One of the angels stepped forward—one of the quieter ones who had been watching us struggle without saying a word. He bent down, waved his hand, and suddenly, the rubble began to shift. The stones and metal pieces floated into the air, rearranging themselves in perfect harmony.

We all watched, mouths hanging open, as the structure rebuilt itself in a matter of seconds. The crooked walls straightened, the wobbly floors leveled out, and by the end of it, we were staring at a sleek, impressive base that looked like it belonged in a sci-fi movie.

"Wait, you could've done that the whole time?" I asked, incredulous.

The angel shrugged. "Figured you needed the practice."

"We nearly died from architectural incompetence!" Akuma cried.

"Maybe next time, don't try to build a base using sarcasm and bad blueprints," the angel said with a smirk. "You're welcome, by the way."

I could only shake my head as we stepped into the new command center. It was everything we could've asked for—and more. The rooms were spacious, the walls were fortified, and best of all, there was a massive screen displaying real-time data on the alien threat. We had our very own high-tech war room.

"Okay," I said, trying to regain some dignity. "This place is awesome. We're definitely saving the world from here."

"And maybe next time," Atticus added, "we can skip the manual labor and just let the angels do the heavy lifting."

I nodded sagely. "Agreed. Now, who's up for s'mores?"

As we stepped into our shiny new command center, the atmosphere shifted. Gone were the worried expressions and grim determination; instead, we were struck by a sense of hope—or maybe it was just the smell of freshly painted walls. Either way, it was a welcome change.

"Okay, team," I said, trying to channel my inner Supreme Commander. "Let's figure out our game plan. We have a war to prepare for, and we need to know what we're up against. First order of business: finding out if our snack supply is adequate."

"Forget snacks," Akuma interrupted, waving a hand like she was swatting away an annoying fly. "What's our first strategy? We need to start training and gathering intel on those aliens."

"Yes, but training and gathering intel are much more enjoyable with snacks," I countered, marching toward the kitchen. "Besides, what kind of warriors are we if we don't have at least one snack break during strategizing?"

"I mean, the best battles are fought on a full stomach," Delver chimed in, following me with an enthusiastic nod. "And marshmallows count as a legitimate food group, right?"

The kitchen was surprisingly equipped, stocked with everything from magical fruit that sparkled like they were having a disco party to a suspicious-looking pot that claimed to brew anything from coffee to "Liquid Victory." Atticus eyed the pot warily.

"Just don't try to brew anything too crazy," he said, raising an eyebrow. "Last time we ended up with a potion that made everyone speak in rhymes for three days straight."

"I thought it was hilarious," Akuma grinned. "I could've gotten used to calling you 'the fearless warrior of funky hats.'"

"Maybe I should just brew a potion that makes you all want to help me cook," Atticus muttered, shoving his hands into his pockets.

We grabbed an assortment of snacks and migrated to the central room, which had a massive round table surrounded by high-backed chairs that screamed "serious business." I plopped down, arranging the snacks like they were important pieces on a game board.

"Okay, first things first," I said, pulling up a holographic map of the surrounding area on the center screen. "We need to know what we're dealing with. Our intel suggests the aliens are... um... well, they're a little intimidating."

"By 'a little intimidating,' you mean 'they can obliterate entire cities with a sneeze,' right?" Atticus asked, munching on a glittering grape that looked like it had survived an explosion.

"Exactly," I nodded, feeling my enthusiasm wane slightly. "And we don't even have good intel on their technology or tactics. It's like trying to fight a dragon armed with nothing but a feather duster."

"Or a marshmallow catapult," Akuma suggested with a smirk. "But hey, marshmallows would at least be a fun distraction!"

"Right," I said, suppressing a grin. "But I think we need to approach this a little more strategically."

Delver tapped the map, and it zoomed in on an area labeled "Alien Encampment." "What if we use our respective factions to gather intel? The Dragons can go airborne, the Phoenixes can explode stuff for distraction, the Griffins can charge in for frontline action, and the Serpents can—"

"Be all sneaky and stealthy," Akuma interjected. "I see what you're doing here. We split into teams and gather as much info as we can without getting turned into space goo."

"Sounds like a plan!" I declared, and suddenly felt a rush of excitement. "And we'll get to show off our awesome new base! Who knows, maybe we can impress the aliens with our magnificent teamwork."

"That'll definitely confuse them," Atticus said, rolling his eyes. "But seriously, we need to be smart about this. We don't want to get caught off guard."

I nodded, all traces of humor vanishing as I considered the implications. "Agreed. But we also have to make sure we don't get too wrapped up in being serious. We need morale."

"Right," Delver added, crossing his arms. "So, we'll have to do a combination of training and team-building exercises. You know, like trust falls, but with fireballs."

I grimaced at the thought. "Yeah, because trust falls have always ended well for me."

"Maybe we can add in some friendly competitions!" Akuma chimed in, her eyes sparkling with mischief. "Like races or who can make the best fireball display. That'll keep things lively."

"Perfect!" I exclaimed. "And we can reward the winners with the best snacks!"

As the plan unfolded, the mood in the room shifted to one of excitement. We were warriors, but we were also friends. And while we had a war to prepare for, it was the bonds we formed and the laughter we shared that would help carry us through the tough times.

Three Days Later

Our first training day arrived with an unexpected twist: a surprise guest. As we lined up for what was supposed to be an intense workout session, a tall figure stepped through the entrance, dressed in a shiny suit of armor that sparkled like it was still under warranty.

"Who are you?" I asked, eyeing the newcomer with suspicion. "You look like a character out of a really cheesy space opera."

"I am Zorak," he announced, striking a pose that made him look like he was auditioning for a Broadway musical. "And I am here to train you in the ancient arts of combat!"

"Okay, but can you keep the sparkles to a minimum?" Atticus quipped. "We're trying to be serious warriors here, not a parade float."

Zorak chuckled, clearly undeterred. "Seriousness is overrated! Let us dance, my friends! Dance with power!"

"Dance? Oh no, not the dance training," I groaned. "I thought we were here to learn to fight, not to compete in Dancing with the Stars."

As Zorak began leading us through a series of bizarre yet oddly effective combat dances, we couldn't help but laugh at how absurd it all was. Sure, we were supposed to be preparing for an alien invasion, but at least we were doing it with style.

And as we whirled and spun like a bunch of bewildered flamingos, I realized something important: sometimes, it wasn't about the training itself but the camaraderie that formed in the process. And maybe, just maybe, we'd be ready for whatever the aliens threw our way.

I could already picture it: a group of fierce warriors battling it out while performing the latest dance craze. It would go down in history—if we survived long enough to write it down, that is.

"Well, if nothing else, we'll definitely confuse our enemies," Akuma said, grinning.

And at that moment, with laughter ringing through our new base, I knew we were ready to face whatever challenges awaited us. We might not have all the answers yet, but we had each other. And in the face of an alien apocalypse, that was a powerful weapon in its own right.

CHAPTER SEVEN

Dancing with Aliens (Not Quite)

Okay, so if someone had told me that my first week in this shiny new command center would involve an intergalactic dance-off with a character straight out of a B-movie, I would have laughed so hard I'd have to check my vibrational frequency. But here we were, surrounded by gleaming equipment and the distant sounds of combat training, all while Zorak led us through what he insisted was an essential combat technique: the Galactic Groove.

"Now, my warriors," Zorak proclaimed, striking yet another dramatic pose, "we will combine the art of war with the art of dance!"

I glanced around at my friends. Atticus had his arms crossed, eyebrows raised as if trying to communicate his disbelief without uttering a word. Akuma was furiously trying to copy Zorak's moves while simultaneously cracking jokes. Delver looked utterly confused, which wasn't entirely unusual for him. And then there was me, stuck between a laugh and a groan.

"Alright, troops!" I shouted, trying to regain control of this absurd situation. "Remember, we're here to train for an alien invasion, not to audition for a space-themed reality show!"

"Speak for yourself!" Akuma retorted, twirling with wild abandon. "This could be my big break!"

"Sure, just wait until you're dodging laser blasts while trying to do the cha-cha," Atticus shot back. "Not exactly the safest dance partner."

As we clumsily attempted to follow Zorak's "Galactic Groove," I noticed something strange: our movements were more coordinated than I'd expected. Maybe it was the sheer ridiculousness of the situation that brought us closer together, but even as we flailed around, there was an undeniable sense of unity.

"Okay, focus!" I yelled, throwing my hands in the air dramatically. "Dance practice is all fine and dandy, but we need to tackle actual training next! And by actual training, I mean... uh... who's up for a little obstacle course?"

Zorak's eyes lit up like he'd just been told there was free pizza. "Obstacle course? Yes! A challenge worthy of the Galactic Warriors!"

I rolled my eyes, but secretly felt a surge of excitement. The obstacle course was set up in the sprawling backyard of the command center. It had everything: laser beams, balance beams, mud pits, and something that looked suspiciously like a giant inflatable dragon. I made a mental note to inquire about that later.

"Here's the plan," I said, pacing in front of my friends. "We split into teams. Akuma and Atticus versus Delver and me. Let's see who can finish the course the fastest!"

"Not if I can help it," Akuma declared, striking a superhero pose as if she were the main character in her own action movie.

"Bring it on!" Delver shot back, his competitive side coming out. I had to admit, there was something invigorating about the idea of racing against my friends. It made the looming alien invasion seem just a little less intimidating.

"On your marks, get set... GO!" I shouted, and we were off, charging toward the obstacle course like we were in a race for the last slice of pizza at a party.

As we dove into the first obstacle—an elaborate web of laser beams—I couldn't help but feel like I was in a video game. "Remember," I yelled over my shoulder, "don't touch the lasers! Or you'll get zapped like a pancake on a grill!"

"Thanks for the heads up, Captain Obvious!" Atticus shot back, expertly dodging a beam.

With a surge of adrenaline, I dove under the first laser and rolled to my feet, narrowly avoiding a second one. Behind me, I heard Delver yelp as he misjudged his jump and got his foot caught in the mud pit.

"Delver! What did I tell you about watching where you're going?" I laughed, trying not to trip over my own feet.

"I'm multitasking!" he exclaimed, trying to extract his foot while flailing like an awkward marionette. "I can't watch and run at the same time!"

Meanwhile, Akuma and Atticus were ahead, navigating the course like seasoned ninjas. They were a blur of movement, but just as they approached the inflatable dragon, disaster struck. Atticus slipped, and it was like watching a slow-motion disaster unfold.

"NO!" I shouted, waving my arms as if I could somehow halt time.

He careened into the inflatable dragon, and it let out a ridiculous squeaking sound, like a deflating balloon. The entire obstacle course seemed to pause for a moment, all eyes on Atticus as he clung to the dragon like it was his last hope of salvation.

"I meant to do that!" he hollered, even as he flopped dramatically to the ground, rolling in the mud.

Akuma laughed so hard she almost toppled over. "Yeah, right! You look like a deflated knight!"

"Guys, we're supposed to be training, not providing the comedy act for the intergalactic talent show!" I called out, trying to keep my laughter in check.

After what felt like an eternity of giggles, mud, and the occasional squeak of the inflatable dragon, we finally crossed the finish line—barely able to breathe from laughing so hard. Zorak appeared, somehow managing to look regal despite being covered in mud.

"Excellent work, my warriors!" he boomed, pumping his fists in the air like he was announcing the world's greatest dance party. "You have embraced the spirit of Galactic Groove! Now, let us feast!"

The "feast" turned out to be a hodgepodge of snacks that ranged from edible glitter to some very suspicious-looking blue goo that Atticus declared was "definitely not food."

As we munched on our prizes, I couldn't help but feel a swell of gratitude for my friends. Sure, we were training for a war, but we were doing it together, one ridiculous moment at a time.

Just then, the ground shook. I looked around, alarmed. "Did anyone else feel that?"

"Uh-oh," Delver said, looking slightly green. "If the aliens are launching their attack, I hope they come bearing snacks."

I shot him a look. "That's not the point, genius! Something's happening!"

And then, from the corner of my eye, I spotted a glimmering object flying toward us, leaving a trail of sparkling dust behind it. My heart raced as the object drew closer, revealing itself to be... a holographic message.

"Great," I muttered, watching as it flickered to life. "What fresh chaos is this?"

A figure appeared, cloaked in shadows but radiating an eerie glow. "Eleanor, Atticus, Akuma, Delver—your training is just beginning. Prepare yourselves. The invasion has begun... and you are the key."

And with that cryptic warning, the message flickered out, leaving us staring at each other in a mix of confusion and disbelief.

"Well," I said finally, trying to shake off the feeling of impending doom, "that was... cheerful. Who's up for round two of Galactic Groove?"

"Do we have to?" Atticus groaned. "I think I've had enough dancing for a lifetime."

"Just remember," I said with a grin, "we're in this together. And if we're going to face whatever's coming, we might as well do it with style. Or at least with some really good snacks."

And so, we plunged back into our dance training, laughter echoing through the command center, even as the specter of the alien threat loomed closer. Because if there was one thing I knew for sure, it was that humor would be our greatest weapon in the war to come.

Two months had passed since our embarrassing dance-off turned obstacle course catastrophe. In that time, we had trained harder than any video game character facing a final boss—fighting off endless waves of mock aliens while dodging inflatable dragons and consuming snacks that were definitely a health hazard.

The command center had become a second home, complete with questionable décor that would make even the most patient interior designer weep. I mean, who thought it was a good idea to hang a giant inflatable dragon over the main training room? The thing wobbled ominously whenever someone sneezed, and I'd half-expected it to come to life and start demanding tribute.

As we pushed through our routines, my friends began to develop their own unique quirks. Atticus, for example, had taken to wearing an assortment of ridiculous headgear during training sessions. One day it was a pirate hat, the next a Viking helmet complete with plastic horns. "It's all about channeling my inner warrior!" he proclaimed, adjusting his latest look—an oversized sombrero—while striking a pose that made him look more like a circus clown than a battle-hardened hero.

Akuma, on the other hand, had developed a knack for dramatic entrances. She'd dramatically burst through doors, windows, or, on one occasion, an air vent, shouting, "Fear not, for I have arrived!" The day she burst through the door in a superhero cape—which, if I was honest, was just a bedsheet—was both impressive and concerning. "I can't believe you just climbed through an air vent," I laughed, shaking my head as she dusted off her "cape." "What if you got stuck?"

"Pssh! As if!" she shot back, tossing her hair over her shoulder. "I'm basically a ninja! They don't get stuck in vents! They glide!"

Delver, our beloved (and sometimes confused) brooding warrior, had developed a rather unexpected passion for gardening. "Look, Eleanor," he said one day, proudly presenting a potted plant that looked suspiciously like it had come from a Jurassic Park sequel. "This is a Venus flytrap. I think it can help us in battle!"

I blinked at the plant. "You think we're going to use a plant to defeat aliens? What's next, Delver? Are we summoning the power of nature to vanquish our foes?"

"Yes!" he declared, with all the seriousness of someone who had just been handed the fate of the universe. "We will use its hunger for victory to outsmart our enemies!"

Meanwhile, I was just trying to survive training and prepare for whatever the universe threw our way. We spent our days switching between hand-to-hand combat drills, dance-offs that somehow became more competitive, and mock battles that often ended with someone getting stuck in the inflatable dragon (looking at you, Atticus).

On a particularly chaotic afternoon, Zorak decided we needed to practice our teamwork by attempting to build a defensive wall out of, you guessed it, inflatable dragons. "This will be an excellent test of your skills!" he proclaimed, oblivious to the chaos that would inevitably ensue.

"Right, because nothing screams 'defense' like a wall of bouncy, inflatable beasts," I muttered under my breath as I helped Akuma inflate another dragon. "This feels like a poorly executed party idea rather than a military strategy."

"Just you wait!" Akuma replied, her eyes sparkling with mischief. "When those aliens show up, they'll be so distracted by our fabulous décor that they won't know what hit them!"

Little did we know, Zorak had planned this entire exercise as a way to prepare us for the unexpected—like, say, if we had to face an actual alien invasion with nothing but inflatable dragons and our sheer will to survive.

As we began assembling our wall, laughter filled the air. "Guys!" I shouted over the sound of squeaking inflatables. "Remember, the goal is to build a wall, not a giant bouncy castle!"

"Too late!" Atticus yelled from the back, where he was engaged in a personal battle with an inflatable dragon that had apparently decided to take on a life of its own. "This is a full-on castle! We could host a birthday party in here!"

"Yeah, a birthday party with a side of imminent doom!" I shot back, shaking my head. "Is that really how we want to go down in history?"

After a few more hours of inflatable chaos and borderline insanity, we finally managed to erect our "defensive wall." It leaned slightly to the left and squeaked ominously, but it stood—if you squinted and ignored the fact that it looked more like a toddler's play structure than an actual defense.

"That's one impressive wall!" Zorak declared, nodding in approval. "Now, let's test its durability!"

"Please tell me we're not actually going to attack it," I groaned. "I mean, what's next? Should we throw cupcakes at it to test its resistance?"

"Excellent idea!" Zorak exclaimed, waving his arms enthusiastically. "We shall prepare an onslaught of cupcakes!"

"Zorak, you're insane," I muttered, shaking my head. "And I'm pretty sure we'll be using actual weapons against aliens soon."

As we braced ourselves for the inevitable cupcake assault, I couldn't help but marvel at how far we'd come in such a short time. Training wasn't just about becoming warriors; it was about forging bonds and laughter in the face of impending doom.

Just as the first wave of cupcakes was launched at our inflatable wall, the ground trembled once more, shaking the very foundations of our makeshift fortress. I froze, my heart racing.

"Was that just me, or is something big coming?" Delver asked, glancing nervously at the shaking walls.

"No, that was definitely a thing," I replied, my heart pounding. "Something's happening!"

And with that ominous thought hanging over us, we prepared to face whatever chaos awaited. Because if history had taught us anything, it was that when the universe threw you into the deep end, you better learn to swim—or at least float on inflatable dragons.

CHAPTER EIGHT

The Ground Shakes, the Cake Flakes

Just when we thought our inflatable dragon fortress was secure—made more secure by an impressive, albeit highly questionable, cupcake fortification—the ground decided it was time for a little shake-up. As the tremors rumbled beneath us, it was as if the Earth itself was auditioning for a part in a horror movie, complete with dramatic music and a surprise monster reveal.

"Alright, team!" Zorak shouted, clearly loving this moment way too much. "Time for a battle plan! I need your attention!"

We all gathered, adrenaline pumping and icing from the cupcakes still smudged on our faces. "This better be good," I muttered, wiping frosting from my cheek. "Because I just launched a cupcake at Delver and it was not pretty."

"Hey!" Delver protested, wiping crumbs off his shirt, "That was a strategically placed distraction! I was preparing for battle!"

"Right, with frosting and sprinkles," I snorted, shaking my head. "Very intimidating."

"Enough about cake! Focus!" Zorak commanded, dramatically spreading his arms like he was about to take flight. "We have an unprecedented situation! The ground is shaking, and we must prepare for whatever comes next!"

Just as I was about to ask how we were supposed to prepare when we were all covered in frosting, the earth shook violently again. This time, it was followed by a loud rumble that echoed through our makeshift training ground. The inflatable dragons shuddered, as if they too were feeling the impending doom.

"I think we should abandon the fortress!" Akuma yelled, eyes wide with excitement and just a hint of panic. "Unless this is part of the training!"

"It's definitely not part of the training!" I yelled back, glancing at our crumbling wall. "We've gone from warriors to pastry chefs overnight!"

"Everyone to your positions!" Zorak bellowed, thrusting a finger dramatically toward the entrance. "We stand together, ready for whatever may come!"

With that, we rushed toward the exit, adrenaline coursing through our veins, fueled by a mix of fear and pure chocolate cake frosting. Just outside, we were greeted by the sight of a massive fissure splitting the ground open, like the Earth was deciding to take a nap and roll over.

"Alright, time for a field trip!" Atticus shouted, clutching a plastic sword that had seen better days. "Let's go see what's down there!"

"Right, because what could possibly go wrong?" I deadpanned, rolling my eyes. "Next, you'll suggest we take a selfie with whatever's down there."

As we approached the crack in the Earth, we all stared into the abyss. From its depths came a low growl, echoing like a disgruntled cat after being woken up too early.

"Is that... is that a dinosaur?" Akuma whispered, her voice trembling with excitement. "Or a dragon? Or maybe it's a giant cupcake monster!"

"A giant cupcake monster?" I couldn't help but laugh. "If it's a giant cupcake monster, I'm definitely making a run for it. I'm not ready to be devoured by baked goods!"

"Focus, people!" Zorak snapped, trying to regain control of the situation. "We need to assess the threat!"

Before we could even prepare for a cupcake catastrophe or a giant dinosaur, a head popped up from the crack. It was massive, covered in scales, with a toothy grin that looked suspiciously like it had just been to a dentist who specialized in getting people's hopes up.

"Hello!" the creature boomed, sounding both cheerful and terrifying. "I'm Gerald! I've been sleeping down here for a thousand years. Sorry if I startled you!"

"Um, excuse me?" I blinked, utterly dumbfounded. "You've been sleeping down there? Are you a dragon? Or an ancient guardian of some kind?"

"Eh, more of a 'giant who really enjoys naps.'" Gerald shrugged, his scales glimmering in the sunlight. "But yes, I have some ancient wisdom. I can help you prepare for the aliens! But first, can someone get me a sandwich? I haven't eaten since the last Ice Age!"

"What kind of sandwich do you want?" Delver asked, stepping forward like he was trying to win the creature over with his culinary expertise.

"Turkey with a side of existential dread," Gerald replied nonchalantly, as if ordering from a diner. "And don't forget the pickles!"

"I can't believe I'm asking this, but we'll get you a sandwich if you help us!" I blurted out, still trying to wrap my head around a giant creature named Gerald asking for lunch.

"Deal!" Gerald replied, beaming at us with a smile that was too big for his face. "But first, I need to see what you're up against. This whole 'aliens are coming' thing has my scales all ruffled."

"Welcome to the club," I muttered under my breath. "We're all a little ruffled."

As the ground continued to shake and the reality of an ancient giant being our only hope settled in, I couldn't help but feel a surge of camaraderie among my friends. We had made it this far, battling frosting-covered obstacles, and now we were teaming up with a massive creature named Gerald for a sandwich and possibly a showdown with whatever was lurking beyond the fissure.

"Alright, team!" Zorak shouted, his voice booming over the rumbling ground. "Gerald, I'm counting on you! Let's figure out how to prepare for this impending doom and maybe get some sandwiches in the process!"

And with that, we set off to explore this bizarre twist of fate, laughing in the face of danger—or at least trying to distract ourselves from the fact that we were about to embark on an adventure that involved a giant and possibly a dozen sandwiches.

As we stood there, staring at Gerald the giant, I could practically hear the gears in Delver's head turning. "So... you were asleep for a thousand years, and you're just waking up now?" he asked, trying to wrap his mind around the situation like it was a particularly challenging puzzle.

"Yep! A nice, cozy nap!" Gerald exclaimed, stretching his enormous arms wide. "I just woke up, saw the ground shaking, and thought, 'Hey, this seems like a good time to see what the kids are up to!' But I'm not here to just hang out. I want to help!"

"Help us? With what? Lunch orders?" Akuma quipped, raising an eyebrow.

"Very funny," Gerald chuckled, rolling his eyes. "No, I can help you with your preparations for the aliens! I've seen things, kiddo. Things that would make your hair stand on end—wait, do you even have hair?" He paused, looking at my now-white locks. "Oh, right. Nice style!"

"Thanks, Gerald," I said, feigning nonchalance. "I like to think it's in right now. But can we focus on the impending alien invasion? What do you know about them?"

"Not much, but I did overhear some interesting stuff from the last group of explorers who passed through." Gerald leaned in, lowering his voice conspiratorially, though given his size, it was more like he was lowering a mountain. "They talked about some high-tech gadgets and weird creatures that can turn invisible. Real nasty business. You need a solid plan!"

"A solid plan? Like building a cupcake fortress?" I deadpanned, gesturing dramatically at our jiggling bouncy wall behind us.

"Ugh, please don't remind me," Akuma groaned. "We need something a little more serious than our 'edible defense.'"

"Right, so what's the plan, Gerald?" Atticus asked, adjusting his sombrero and attempting to appear serious, which was a hilarious sight considering we were literally standing in front of a giant.

"Well, you'll need an army. And by 'army,' I don't mean a bunch of kids playing pretend. You need real warriors, and I can help you train them!" he declared, excitement lighting up his colossal face.

"Great! So we just find an army?" I asked, raising an eyebrow. "You make it sound easy."

Gerald chuckled, his laughter rumbling through the ground. "You have the makings of a good leader, Eleanor! Now, let's strategize. You've got those faction leaders, right?"

"Yes!" I said, nodding enthusiastically. "There's me with the Dragons, Atticus with Hell, Akuma with Avian, and Delver with Phoenix."

"Awesome! But you'll need a few more peeps if you want to stand a chance. I have friends, you know—giants like me, trolls, and some other weird folks. Just... don't ask too many questions." Gerald raised a finger. "Trust me. Some of them might be more interested in sandwiches than war."

"Are you sure they won't be too friendly?" Delver asked cautiously. "I mean, what if they show up and just want to hang out?"

"Yeah, because that's what you want—giant trolls at your party," I chimed in. "I can see the banner now: 'Welcome to the party, please bring snacks and a lot of patience!'"

"Exactly!" Gerald said, nodding seriously. "But I promise they're not all about snacks. Some can fight! We can turn your cupcake fortress into a stronghold!"

"I'd prefer it if we could skip the cupcakes altogether," Akuma muttered, crossing her arms. "But I guess if it involves more dragons and less frosting, I'm in."

"Great! You just need to gather your leaders, and I'll send out a call to my giant buddies. They love a good adventure!" Gerald said, excitement bubbling in his deep voice. "But first, can we get that sandwich?"

"Of course!" Atticus replied, clapping his hands together. "Let's take a break to get Gerald his turkey sandwich. I'm sure that's vital for our battle plans!"

So, we trooped back into the command center, determined to find the biggest sandwich we could. As we rummaged through the makeshift kitchen—complete with questionable-looking leftovers—Gerald explained his plans to gather the troops.

"Remember, teamwork is key!" he said, munching happily on the sandwich we eventually threw together, which looked suspiciously like it had been assembled by a committee of four-year-olds. "You need to convince them that you're worth fighting for!"

"Got it! We'll present ourselves as the dream team!" I said, stuffing my face with half a sandwich, trying to sound as inspiring as possible. "With a side of baked goods!"

"Or we could make them super jealous of our cool inflatable fortress!" Akuma chimed in, grinning. "I mean, who wouldn't want to be part of the cupcake squad?"

"Cupcake squad? We're trying to prepare for an alien invasion, not a baking contest!" I protested, laughing as I took a bite. "But honestly, if we survive this, I'm totally throwing a giant cake party."

Just as we settled into our plan of making friends and fighting aliens, the ground shook again. This time it felt more like a roar than a rumble.

"Okay, seriously, is this the earthquake episode of our lives?" Atticus joked, eyes wide. "What's next, a giant hand reaching up to give us a high-five?"

"Why don't we all just say 'hello' to the ground before we go insane?" Delver suggested, half-laughing, half-nervous. "I'm pretty sure it's trying to communicate."

"Whatever it is, let's not stick around to find out!" I said, rallying my friends. "We have a plan, and it involves epic sandwiches, a giant, and maybe even some fighting practice with our new troops!"

And with that, we decided to embrace whatever was shaking up our world. Because if we were going to battle aliens and possibly survive a giant sandwich party, we might as well do it with a sense of humor—and a cupcake or two.

CHAPTER NINE

When the Ground Shakes, We Brace for Impact

The next morning felt different. The air had a tense quality, as if it were holding its breath, waiting for something momentous to happen. I stood at the edge of our inflatable fortress, looking out over the training grounds where our motley crew was gearing up for the day.

Gerald's call for reinforcements had gone out, and the promise of new allies lingered in the air. But instead of excitement, I felt a knot of anxiety tightening in my stomach. We had been playing pretend for too long, and the reality of our situation was beginning to sink in.

"Hey, Eleanor," Delver said, appearing beside me, his usual grin replaced with a furrowed brow. "You okay? You seem... I don't know, serious."

I sighed, crossing my arms. "I'm just thinking about everything. We're supposed to gather troops, train them, and somehow prepare for an impending alien invasion. It feels a lot like trying to assemble a jigsaw puzzle with missing pieces while standing on a sinking ship."

Delver nodded, a glint of concern in his eyes. "I get that. But we're not in this alone. We have each other, and we have Gerald. Plus, once the giants show up, we'll be ready to fight."

"Ready to fight what, exactly?" I muttered. "We still don't know how powerful our enemies are. I mean, what if they're super advanced and have laser beams that can turn us into cosmic dust?"

"Then we turn into cosmic dust together!" he replied, attempting to inject some levity into my gloom. "But seriously, we need to focus on the training and not get lost in hypotheticals. I mean, we're the greatest warriors of our generation. Right?"

"Right," I said, giving him a half-hearted smile.

"Good! Now, come on, let's get Akuma and Atticus. We need to have a meeting about our strategy before we start freaking out."

"Right, meeting time," I agreed.

As we turned to head back inside, a low rumble shook the ground again, but this time it felt different—more foreboding. My heart raced as I exchanged a worried glance with Delver.

"Did you feel that?" he asked, his eyes narrowing.

"Yeah, definitely."

We pushed through the inflatable door, the squishy material bouncing around us as we stumbled into our makeshift headquarters. Akuma and Atticus were already deep in conversation, pouring over a map sprawled out on a table that looked more like a pizza box than a tactical board.

"Guys," I said, my voice firm, "we need to talk about what just happened outside. It felt... serious."

Atticus looked up, his brow furrowed. "You mean the shaking? I thought that was just Gerald trying to do yoga again."

"I wish it were," I replied, shaking my head. "This felt different—like something was coming."

Akuma leaned forward, her fingers tapping the map with a sense of urgency. "We can't ignore this. We need to prepare for whatever it is, and that means not just gathering troops, but also solidifying our strategies. If we're going to face something unknown, we have to be ready for anything."

Delver stepped closer to the table, examining the map. "Right. We have our factions, but we also need to train together. Dragons, Hell, Avian, and Phoenix need to learn to work as one. If we face an enemy, we can't be divided."

"Agreed," I said, feeling the weight of responsibility pressing on my shoulders. "We'll hold joint training sessions starting today. We can't afford to leave any weaknesses exposed."

"Speaking of weaknesses, let's talk about our strengths," Akuma added. "What do we each bring to the table? Atticus, you're the second most powerful. What's your unique edge?"

"I can control shadows," he said, a spark of confidence igniting in his eyes. "They can be used for stealth, surprise attacks, or creating an illusion. If we can figure out how to make my shadows work together with your dragon fire, we might have a winning combination."

"Now we're talking!" Delver grinned, slapping Atticus on the back. "And what about you, Akuma? You're the leader of the Avian faction. What's your secret weapon?"

She smirked. "I can manipulate wind currents. I've been working on some serious air pressure attacks. Just imagine flying over the battlefield, raining down feathered fury like a vengeful cloud!"

"Sounds badass!" I exclaimed, feeling my spirits lift a little.

"And what about you, Eleanor?" Akuma asked, her gaze sharp. "What's your edge as the Dragon leader?"

"Honestly? I'm still figuring that out," I admitted, feeling the weight of the world on my shoulders again. "I've been focusing on honing my magic and combat skills, but I need to channel my abilities into something more effective for our team."

"Then let's train together!" Delver suggested. "We can figure out how to make your dragon fire more powerful and versatile. We can even come up with some epic battle tactics!"

"Epic battle tactics? Count me in!" I laughed, the tension beginning to ease.

As we brainstormed ideas for joint training sessions and strategies, the ground shook once more, this time a little more violently. I shot a glance at Delver, who grimaced.

"Okay, now that's just rude," he muttered. "It's like the universe is trying to distract us from being awesome!"

"That or something's really coming our way," Akuma replied, her voice steady. "We need to stay vigilant."

Just then, the inflatable door burst open, and Gerald stood in the entrance, panting and slightly out of breath. "I gathered some friends! But they're not... uh, what you'd expect."

"Not what we'd expect?" I echoed, raising an eyebrow.

"Yeah, um, let's just say they might need a little... guidance." Gerald scratched his head. "But they're ready to fight."

"Great! More friends!" I said, feeling the knot in my stomach tighten again. "Just as long as they don't want to have tea parties instead of training."

"Tea parties? That sounds perfect!" Gerald laughed, his voice booming. "But seriously, let's get them in here. We need all the help we can get!"

As we prepared to meet our new recruits, the reality of our situation settled heavily in the air. We were about to face an unknown threat, and I felt the weight of leadership resting firmly on my shoulders.

"Okay, team," I said, raising my voice to rally everyone. "No more jokes! We're going to need every bit of strength, strategy, and teamwork we can muster. The aliens might not be here yet, but we have to act like they are!"

With a collective nod, we steeled ourselves, preparing to face whatever challenges lay ahead.

"After all, if we can handle a giant with a sandwich craving," I said, a grin creeping back onto my face, "we can handle anything!"

And with that, we braced ourselves for the unknown, ready to take on whatever challenges awaited us in the looming shadow of the threat ahead.

The door creaked open wider, and in stepped the "friends" Gerald had mentioned. My initial excitement plummeted faster than a rock in a swimming pool.

The group that followed him was a mix of oddballs. One guy wore a Hawaiian shirt that was so bright it practically screamed, and another had a mohawk that looked like it had been struck by lightning. There was even a girl with a pet ferret peeking out of her backpack, which I had to admit was both adorable and slightly unsettling.

"Everyone, meet our new recruits!" Gerald announced, gesturing like a game show host. "Let's give them a round of applause, or at least a polite nod."

I clapped half-heartedly, unsure how to react.

"Uh, hi?" said the guy in the Hawaiian shirt, clearly nervous. "We're here to help fight the aliens. Or whatever you need."

"Or whatever you need?" I repeated, trying not to laugh. "Great. Just what we need—more ambiguity in a time of impending doom."

"Look," the girl with the ferret said, stepping forward with a spark of determination. "We might not look like much, but we've been training in... unconventional ways. My name's Zara, and this is my battle ferret, Sir Fluffington. He's got mad stealth skills."

"Battle ferret?!" I exclaimed, raising an eyebrow. "Okay, that's officially the coolest thing I've heard all week."

"Believe it or not, he's a fierce little guy," Zara grinned, her ferret squeaking in agreement. "But enough about him! We've got skills! I can manipulate sound waves. Imagine being able to turn up the volume on your opponents' battle cries while whispering sweet nothings to our team."

"Wow, that sounds useful in a chaotic battle," I said, trying to contain my excitement. "What's next? A recruit who can turn invisible while eating pizza?"

"Actually, I can!" piped up the guy in the Hawaiian shirt. "I'm Spencer. I can blend into any background, but only if I'm eating pizza at the time."

I blinked. "Okay, but only if you bring enough for the whole team. That's a rule now."

"Noted!" Spencer beamed, clearly pleased.

"Alright, enough fun. We need to get serious," Akuma said, a slight smirk playing at the corner of her lips. "Welcome to the team, everyone. But we've got training to do. Like, yesterday."

Zara and Spencer exchanged glances, the mood shifting from comedic relief to a more serious tone. "We're ready to train," Zara said, determination back in her eyes. "And Sir Fluffington can help distract the enemy!"

"Yeah, because nothing says 'fear me' like a ferret," Atticus quipped, earning a snicker from the rest of us.

"Don't underestimate the fluff!" Zara shot back. "I've seen him cause confusion and chaos. Sometimes I think he's actually plotting world domination. The ferret, I mean."

"World domination?" Delver laughed. "If he's planning that, we're all in trouble. I mean, I can see the headlines now: 'Humans Defeated by Ferret Army!'"

Just then, the ground shook again, but this time it was more intense. I felt my heart leap into my throat, and the inflatable walls of our HQ shivered ominously.

"What was that?" I gasped, scanning the room.

"Probably just Sir Fluffington's ferret powers," Spencer joked, but the tremor that followed was anything but funny.

"Maybe we should take this seriously," Akuma said, her voice sharp. "Something is definitely going on."

Gerald nodded. "We should gather everyone and head outside. There's something happening, and I can't shake the feeling it's important."

As we rushed outside, the world around us felt charged with energy. The air crackled with tension, and the ground rumbled beneath our feet. I could see other recruits and soldiers hurrying to gather, confusion and concern etched on their faces.

"Everyone, gather around!" I shouted, trying to project authority over the chaos. "We need to regroup and figure out what's happening."

Once we'd all assembled, Gerald stepped forward. "I know we were supposed to focus on training, but something is definitely wrong. The vibrations have been getting stronger, and I have a feeling it's connected to the aliens—or whatever's coming our way."

"You mean it's not just my breakfast burrito?" I asked, half-joking, though the truth settled heavy in my gut.

"Actually, that might be part of it," Delver added, trying to lighten the mood again. "But we need to be prepared for anything."

Suddenly, the ground split open with a thunderous crack, sending everyone stumbling back. A massive plume of dust shot into the air, obscuring our vision.

"Okay, that's not good!" I yelled, pulling my dragon fire to the surface, feeling the familiar rush of power. "Get ready!"

The dust began to settle, and what emerged was not what any of us expected. A massive creature, with scales that shimmered like onyx and eyes glowing like molten gold, rose from the fissure in the earth.

"Well, well, well," it rumbled, voice deep and resonant. "Look at all the little warriors gathered here. How adorable. Did you really think you could prepare without me?"

I blinked, mind racing. "Who are you? Are you friend or foe?"

The creature grinned, sharp teeth glistening. "I'm Kael, a guardian of the realms. And I have come to test your strength."

"Test our strength?" I echoed, incredulous. "Is this some kind of cosmic game show?"

"I think you'll find this test a little more... exhilarating than that."

With a swift movement, Kael raised a clawed hand, and the air around us shimmered with energy. I felt my senses heighten, a surge of adrenaline coursing through my veins.

"Prepare yourselves, children of Earth. Your true battle begins now!"

And just like that, everything shifted.

I glanced at my team, ready to face whatever challenge lay ahead, determination surging within me. If we were going to train and prepare for an uncertain future, we were going to do it right—starting now.

"Alright, team!" I shouted, rallying everyone with renewed vigor. "Looks like we've got a real test on our hands. Let's show Kael what we've got!"

As we stood side by side, ready to face our first true challenge, I couldn't help but think that perhaps this was the moment we had all been waiting for.

And I was more than ready to embrace it.

CHAPTER TEN

Evolving in the Heat of Battle

The ground still trembled beneath us, and Kael stood towering over our group like a walking mountain. The shimmering aura of power surrounding him seemed to echo the very essence of the universe itself.

"Ready or not, here I come!" he bellowed, and before any of us could even think about dodging, he lunged forward, claws glistening in the sunlight.

"Wait! Hold on!" I yelled, my heart racing. "Can't we at least chat about this over coffee first?"

But he wasn't having any of it. His enormous claws swiped through the air, and instinct kicked in. "Everyone, spread out!" I shouted, and we leaped into action, evading the lethal strike just in time.

As I dodged to the side, something remarkable began to happen. The very air around me crackled with energy, and I felt a surge pulse through my body. It was as if the battle itself was awakening dormant power within us, prompting an evolution I hadn't anticipated.

"Eleanor!" Atticus shouted, his voice cutting through the chaos. "I feel it too! This is our chance! We need to be ready for the war to come!"

The air shimmered with magical frequencies, swirling around us as we began to tap into our true potential. The looming threat of the aliens hung over us like a dark cloud, and our evolution felt like the only way to stand a chance.

I felt a warm light envelop me, a kaleidoscope of colors swirling in a harmonious dance. My white hair glowed, shimmering like moonlight, and I could sense a profound change within me. My heart raced as my traits began to crystallize into clear definitions.

Eleanor

Primary Trait: Greatest Dragon

Masterful Mage: My magical abilities heightened, allowing me to manipulate elemental forces at will. I could summon gusts of wind, create barriers of fire, and even conjure illusions to confuse our foes.

Serpentine Sovereignty: I gained control over serpentine creatures, commanding their loyalty and strength. They became my allies in battle, weaving through the chaos like shadows.

Ace Marksman: My precision with ranged attacks was unparalleled, allowing me to hit targets from impossible distances with a flick of my wrist.

Passive Traits:

Vibrational Harmony: My presence resonated with the environment, enhancing my allies' abilities. The closer they were to me, the stronger they felt, as if I amplified their skills.

Dragon's Resilience: I could withstand more damage than ever before, a physical manifestation of my newfound strength.

I turned to see Atticus glowing with a fierce intensity, the golden aura radiating around him like the sun breaking through clouds.

Atticus

Primary Trait: Second Most Powerful

Inferno Wielder: He could summon and control flames, causing them to twist and turn at his command. Fire danced around him, creating a formidable barrier that blazed against our foes.

Heart of a Lion: Atticus's bravery knew no bounds. His presence inspired those around him, instilling a sense of courage that lifted our spirits even in the darkest moments.

Telekinetic Force: With a mere thought, he could move objects around him, creating shields or launching projectiles with impressive force.

Passive Traits:

Flame's Embrace: The heat from his abilities provided warmth and energy to his allies, granting them small boosts in strength and morale.

Phoenix Guardian: Whenever he was injured, a portion of his vitality would transfer to me, ensuring that we remained in the fight together.

Delver stepped forward, his expression determined. A wave of power swept over him, and I could see the transformation unfold.

Delver

Primary Trait: The Phoenix

Skyward Strike: His connection to the skies allowed him to summon powerful storms, using lightning and wind to strike down enemies from above.

Resilient Flight: Delver could glide effortlessly through the air, dodging attacks and repositioning himself in the midst of chaos, making him a slippery target.

Revitalizing Fire: Whenever he unleashed his flames, it healed his allies, wrapping them in a warm, revitalizing energy.

Passive Traits:

Stormcaller: Whenever Delver was present, weather conditions would shift to favor our team, creating protective barriers of wind and rain.

Ever-Rising Spirit: He had an uncanny ability to bounce back from defeats, lifting our spirits and making us more determined to win.

Akuma's energy ignited next, a dark aura swirling around her. She grinned wickedly as she embraced her new powers.

Akuma

Primary Trait: The Avian

Shadow Manipulation: She could meld into shadows, becoming nearly invisible and allowing her to strike from the darkness without warning.

Gale Force: Akuma could summon gusts of wind that knocked enemies off their feet, rendering them vulnerable and confused.

Sonic Screech: A powerful attack that disoriented foes, leaving them dizzy and unable to focus.

Passive Traits:

Cloak of Shadows: Akuma could envelop her allies in shadows, allowing them to become stealthy and undetectable when needed.

Whispers of the Night: Her mere presence heightened her allies' senses, allowing them to hear, see, and feel things they otherwise wouldn't.

As the power surged within us, I glanced back at Kael, who watched us with an amused expression. "Impressive. But let's see if you can back it up!"

"Bring it on!" I shouted, and we charged forward as one, a unified front ready to face the challenges ahead, knowing that our newfound abilities would be critical in our preparations for the impending war.

Kael lunged, and as we moved in sync, a wave of power surged through us. It was exhilarating, electrifying, and most importantly, it felt right. This was what we were meant for—battling together, facing the unknown with courage and laughter.

As we clashed with Kael, the world around us faded, leaving only the thrill of battle, the hum of power, and the indomitable spirit of our newfound abilities. It was a moment of evolution, not just in strength, but in unity and friendship.

"Let's show this guy what we've got!" I shouted, adrenaline coursing through my veins, fueled by the knowledge that we were not just fighting for ourselves, but for the future of humanity.

With renewed energy and determination, we leaped into the fray, ready to prove ourselves and embrace our destinies as warriors preparing for the war that loomed on the horizon.

CHAPTER ELEVEN

You've Got Mail... From Aliens

There's a certain sound an intergalactic message makes when it arrives.

It's not the pleasant ding of a phone notification. No, it's more like the screech of a malfunctioning microwave paired with the groan of a thousand overworked engines. Trust me, you don't ever want to hear it unless you're eager to lose your sanity.

And this morning, I had the joy of waking up to that sound.

"Please tell me that's just the coffee machine," I mumbled as I rubbed the sleep from my eyes. But of course, the room was filled with the hum of tension as everyone stood gathered around the holo-mail, faces pale. Atticus's usual cocky grin was gone, and Akuma looked like she was about to rip the thing in half.

"I think we just got another message from our 'friends,'" Delver said, crossing his arms.

The holo-mail hovered in the air, projecting a swirling mass of digital chaos that eventually formed words, alien characters that shifted into something vaguely readable. My stomach did a backflip as I read the header:

URGENT: PRELIMINARY WAR REPORT

FROM: The Sovereign Armada of Ak'Tuel

TO: All Humans

Oh great. Just what we needed—another friendly letter from the very aliens trying to wipe us off the face of existence.

"Hit play," I said, steeling myself. Delver obliged, tapping the air, and the message expanded, filling the room with cold, emotionless text.

"Humans.

In the grand scheme of universal expansion, you have been deemed unnecessary. This is a courtesy notice to inform you that your planet is now officially a target. We have allowed you time to prepare, but do not mistake this for mercy.

The countdown has begun. Your extinction is inevitable.
Prepare your defenses, not that it will matter.
The Sovereign Armada of Ak'Tuel"

The room fell silent. My heart was pounding. Akuma's eyes were glued to the message, her fingers twitching as though she were imagining squeezing the life out of whoever sent it.

"Unnecessary," Atticus scoffed, breaking the silence with a dry laugh. "Well, that's just rude."

"No kidding," Delver muttered, pacing. "They're giving us a courtesy notice? As if we should thank them for the heads-up."

"I say we hit 'reply all' and tell them where they can shove their message," Akuma growled, her voice laced with venom.

The weight of the words sank in. This wasn't a drill. This wasn't some far-off distant thing we could ignore for a millennium. The aliens were coming, and they weren't going to be polite about it.

"We need to up our game," I said, my voice steady even though my hands shook. "We're evolving, yes, but it's not going to be enough if we don't prepare harder, faster. These aliens... They think they've already won. We can't let them be right."

Atticus gave me a sidelong glance. "And how do you propose we do that? We're already pushing the limits of our training."

I clenched my fists, feeling the raw energy simmer beneath my skin. My powers had grown, no doubt about it, but deep down I knew there was more. More we hadn't even begun to tap into.

"We've got to unlock the next level of our abilities," I said. "I don't care what it takes—we need to dig deeper."

Akuma raised an eyebrow, smirking. "You saying there's more to this evolution than we've been told?"

Delver chimed in, "It's not like the angels handed us a manual. For all we know, there's a whole new set of traits waiting for us once we push hard enough."

"And how exactly do we push hard enough?" Atticus asked, arms folded.

"Simple," I said, the idea crystallizing in my mind. "We have to face death—real, actual danger. We're strong, but we've been holding back because we've never been forced to evolve further. That has to change."

As if on cue, the walls of our base trembled. At first, it felt like an earthquake, a low rumble beneath our feet, but then came the distinct thud of something hitting the ground outside. Something massive.

"Uh... guys," Delver said, voice tight. "I think we've got company."

We rushed outside, the sky darkening as an enormous shadow cast itself over the horizon. A sleek, black metallic ship hovered above us, descending slowly but with the kind of menace you only see in horror movies. The ship was different from anything we'd seen—the design sleek, predatory, and alien. This wasn't part of the war yet, but it sure looked like someone had sent a test.

A trapdoor on the underside of the ship opened, and from it poured dozens—no, hundreds—of mechanical drones, their bodies bristling with weaponry.

"They're sending us a warm-up," I muttered, heart pounding. "Just testing the waters."

Akuma cracked her knuckles, her wings twitching. "Perfect. Let's see how well their tech holds up."

And just like that, chaos erupted.

The drones swarmed us, firing beams of energy and razor-sharp projectiles, but we weren't caught off guard. Akuma dove into the fray, disappearing into the shadows with a wicked grin. One by one, the drones exploded, their circuits fried as she sliced through them like a ghost in the night.

Delver took to the sky, his wings crackling with energy as he summoned a storm above us. Lightning struck down in rapid succession, turning drones into smoking wrecks before they even had a chance to attack.

Atticus was a whirlwind of fire, launching fireballs that incinerated the drones in waves. The ground beneath him scorched as he moved, leaving a trail of ash in his wake. I could hear him laughing—actually laughing—as he dodged between the enemy lines.

And me? Well, I did what I do best. The air hummed with magic as I called forth a barrier, protecting my friends from the initial onslaught, but I could feel it—something pulling at me, deeper power surging just beneath the surface.

This is it, I thought. Now's the time to push past the limits.

I summoned my serpents, their scaled bodies winding through the chaos, snapping up drones and crushing them beneath their jaws. The drones were powerful, but we were more.

But then something shifted. The drones stopped attacking... and regrouped.

"What are they doing?" Atticus called out, his flames flickering as he paused.

"Why do I feel like this is about to get a lot worse?" Delver said, eyeing the drones warily.

The swarm of mechanical enemies suddenly stilled, their red eyes glowing in unison as they shifted into a new formation. The air grew cold. And that's when I saw it—a larger, more ominous drone descending from the ship, its body pulsing with a strange, alien energy.

Oh no.

This one wasn't here to test us. It was here to finish us.

"Everyone, get ready," I said, the tension rising in my chest. "This is going to be one hell of a fight."

There are moments in life where you realize you're seriously outclassed. For most people, it's when they have to parallel park in front of a crowd or attempt advanced calculus.

For us, it was right about now.

The massive drone descended from the mothership, landing with a bone-rattling thud. It towered over us, easily three stories tall, its metallic body covered in what looked like alien glyphs glowing with an eerie blue light. Its eyes locked onto us, and I swear I saw the faintest smirk—if a giant murder-bot could smirk, that is.

"What's the plan, Eleanor?" Atticus asked, flames crackling in his hands. His usual cocky demeanor was still there, but I could tell he was taking this seriously. He didn't have a choice.

"Plan? Who said we have a plan?" I shot back, eyes scanning the enemy for weaknesses.

Delver, hovering midair, shouted down, "How about not dying for starters?"

Akuma reappeared beside me, her wings twitching. "That's a given. But how do we take this thing down? If the little guys were this tough, what's that thing packing?"

As if answering her question, the drone's chest opened up, revealing a swirling mass of energy. Without warning, it unleashed a pulse that rippled through the air like a sonic boom, knocking us all off our feet.

Note to self: avoid giant glowing core of death.

I scrambled to my feet, but my legs felt like jelly. That pulse hadn't just knocked us down—it had drained our energy. My magic felt sluggish, like trying to run through quicksand.

"Not good," Delver groaned from above, his wings faltering. "It's messing with our powers."

Atticus snarled, flames sparking weakly in his palms. "What the hell are we supposed to do if we can't use our abilities?"

I took a deep breath, trying to center myself. There has to be a way. Think, Eleanor, think.

That's when I remembered what I'd said earlier—about pushing ourselves beyond our limits. We'd never faced a real, genuine threat like this. Maybe... just maybe... this was the moment.

"Okay, new plan," I said, standing tall, even though my knees wobbled. "We don't hold back. This thing is forcing us to play safe. We need to stop doing that."

Akuma looked at me like I'd lost it. "You want us to go all out while this thing's draining us? Are you insane?"

"No," I said, eyes narrowing at the giant drone. "I'm just ready to stop playing small."

Without waiting for a reply, I focused all my remaining energy, summoning my serpents. But instead of the usual two or three, I pushed for more—more than I'd ever called before. Pain flared in my chest, but I gritted my teeth and kept going.

Six serpents burst from the ground, their scales gleaming like molten silver, their eyes burning with unbridled fury. They circled the drone, hissing as they prepared to strike.

"Whoa," Delver said, wide-eyed. "Since when can you do that?"

I didn't answer. There wasn't time. I pointed toward the drone, and my serpents launched themselves forward, fangs bared.

The drone retaliated, firing a barrage of energy beams, but my serpents weaved through the air, dodging with impossible speed. They struck, coiling around the drone's legs and squeezing with bone-crushing force.

Atticus, catching on to the idea, grinned and summoned every ounce of fire he had left, shaping it into a massive flaming spear. "If we're going down, we're going down swinging!" he shouted before launching the spear directly at the drone's glowing core.

The spear flew through the air, leaving a trail of fire in its wake. The drone, distracted by my serpents, didn't react fast enough. The spear hit the core dead-on, and for a second, time seemed to freeze.

Then, there was an explosion.

The force of it sent us all flying backward, but this time, it wasn't the same draining pulse. No, this was the sound of victory—however small.

The dust settled, and the drone stood motionless, sparks flying from its core. My serpents slithered back toward me, their job done.

"We... we did it," Delver said, panting as he touched down beside me.

The drone's chest cavity sparked one last time before it finally collapsed, hitting the ground with an earth-shaking crash.

Akuma let out a breath she'd been holding. "Remind me never to doubt you again."

I managed a weak smile. "Only if you promise to stop underestimating yourself."

Atticus walked up, his usual swagger returning. "You know, I'm kind of impressed we're still alive. I was fully prepared to go out in a blaze of glory."

"I don't know about glory," I said, "but we're definitely not out of the woods yet."

As if on cue, another sound filled the air—this time a low, rumbling noise. I glanced up at the massive mothership still looming overhead. The trapdoor was opening again.

"Oh, come on," Delver groaned. "Can we get a break once?"

"Doesn't look like it," I muttered.

But something was different this time. Instead of another wave of drones, a sleek, metallic pod dropped from the ship, landing with a soft thud in the distance. It was smaller, more discreet, and much more ominous.

"What is that?" Akuma asked, eyes narrowing.

"No idea," I said, my pulse quickening. "But I've got a bad feeling about it."

The pod hissed, releasing a cloud of steam as it began to open. For a moment, nothing happened.

Then, from within the pod, a figure emerged—humanoid but unmistakably alien. Its body was covered in gleaming silver armor, its eyes glowing with the same eerie blue light as the drones. It stood tall, radiating an aura of authority, like it wasn't just any soldier but someone... important.

"Is that...?" Delver started, but his voice trailed off.

The figure stepped forward, surveying us with cold, calculating eyes. Then, without a word, it raised one hand—and the ground beneath us trembled.

"Oh, great," Atticus muttered, gripping his sword tightly. "We just can't catch a break, can we?"

The figure's eyes flickered, and suddenly I felt it—a pressure, like something was gripping my mind, squeezing. It wasn't physical, but it was there, invading my thoughts, probing.

I staggered, clutching my head. "It's... in my mind..."

"Same here," Akuma said through gritted teeth. "I can feel it trying to—"

Before she could finish, the alien spoke, its voice echoing inside our heads.

"Humans. You are stronger than anticipated. But your resistance is futile. You cannot stop what is coming."

I glanced at the others, feeling the weight of its words.

"We'll see about that," I muttered, focusing all my energy to push back against the mental invasion.

But deep down, I knew this was only the beginning.

CHAPTER TWELVE

Science Fiction Meets Medieval Magic

If you'd told me a year ago that I'd be standing in a sci-fi laboratory that looked like something straight out of a space movie while planning the defense of Earth from an alien invasion, I would've laughed in your face. But here I was, surrounded by glowing consoles, floating holograms, and more flashing lights than a Christmas parade.

Welcome to the Dragon Faction's Research Institute—officially known as Draconis Lab. The place was a mix of medieval fantasy aesthetics and cutting-edge technology. Imagine a stone-walled fortress, complete with glowing runes, but instead of swords and shields, we had tech straight out of the future.

"Eleanor, can you stop ogling the giant floating sphere of plasma for a second?" Delver called out from across the lab, where he was tinkering with what looked like some kind of energy rifle. His fingers flew over the buttons like he'd been a weapons engineer his whole life.

I blinked and tore my gaze away from the massive containment unit in the middle of the room. Inside, a glowing sphere hovered, rotating lazily in the air. It was plasma—the kind that could fry you to a crisp if you even thought about touching it. The Dragon faction had been working on turning it into some kind of ultra-powered weapon. Nothing too over-the-top, just your average planet-destroying energy bomb. No big deal.

"What? I'm just appreciating the scenery," I replied, rolling my eyes. "It's not every day you see a magical, glowing ball of potential death."

"Don't touch it," Atticus warned, appearing beside me. His white hair was messy from staying up too late, probably running simulations. "Last time someone messed with it, we had to rebuild half the lab."

“That was your fault,” Delver chimed in with a smirk, leaning casually against the workbench. “And it was only a quarter of the lab, tops.”

Atticus crossed his arms. “I didn’t see you volunteering to help rebuild it.”

“Guys,” I interrupted, rubbing my temples. “Focus. We’ve got bigger problems than who broke what.”

Akuma flew down from the second-floor balcony, her wings retracting gracefully as she landed. “She’s right. Besides, I’m tired of babysitting you two.”

I raised an eyebrow. “Babysitting?”

“Yeah. Someone has to make sure you don’t accidentally blow up the planet before the aliens even get here,” she teased.

We all gathered around the central console, where holographic blueprints of the lab hovered in mid-air. Each faction had its own research institute, but Draconis Lab was the crown jewel. Of course, I was biased. The other factions had impressive facilities too, but ours just had that extra flair, you know? I mean, plasma containment units and magical enhancements? You couldn’t beat that.

“I’ve been keeping an eye on the other factions,” Delver said, his eyes narrowing as he brought up the other research facilities on the hologram. “The Serpent faction’s institute is making serious progress with their stealth tech. Their cloaking devices are nearly undetectable.”

“That’s no surprise,” Atticus muttered. “The Serpents are all about sneaking around.”

Akuma frowned, tapping the air to pull up Phoenix Lab’s blueprints. “And Phoenix Faction? They’re experimenting with explosive attacks. Not just magical ones, either. They’re merging fire magic with tech-based warheads. The results are... explosive.”

“Great,” I sighed. “So we’ve got cloaking tech from the Serpents, explosive warheads from the Phoenixes, and who knows what the Avians are cooking up.”

Delver pulled up the hologram for the Avian Faction’s institute—Griffonworks. “The Avians are focusing on physical enhancements. Their soldiers are getting faster, stronger, more durable. I heard they’ve got exoskeleton suits now.”

“Awesome,” I said, my voice dripping with sarcasm. “So basically, we’re all working on things that could either save or obliterate the planet. Cool, cool.”

"Hey, it's not all bad," Atticus said, clapping me on the back. "At least we're making progress."

Progress was one way to put it. Every faction had its own specialized research institute, each one designed to push the boundaries of magic and science to their absolute limits. While the Serpents worked on stealth and espionage, the Phoenixes focused on high-impact attacks, and the Avians perfected physical combat enhancements.

As for us Dragons? We were the tech-magicians, blending the best of both worlds.

"I think we need to check in with the other factions," I said, crossing my arms. "Make sure we're all on the same page before the next big battle."

"Good idea," Delver agreed. "The last thing we need is some giant miscommunication in the middle of a fight."

Akuma grinned. "Or worse. One of their experiments backfiring. I don't trust half the stuff the Phoenixes are playing with."

"Can't argue with that," Atticus said, nodding. "Let's go check out what everyone's up to."

We left Draconis Lab and made our way to the other factions' institutes. First up: Serpent Covert Ops. The place was hidden underground, obviously. You'd never know it was there unless you were looking for it—and even then, good luck.

The lab was sleek, dark, and almost ominous, with holographic walls that changed color depending on your movement. It was unsettling, but that's exactly how the Serpents liked it.

We were greeted by Kian, the head of the Serpent faction. He gave us a smirk as we entered. "I see you've come to admire our work."

"More like checking to make sure you're not building doomsday devices," I said, only half-joking.

Kian's grin widened. "Don't worry, Eleanor. Our work here is purely... strategic."

I raised an eyebrow. "Uh-huh. And what 'strategic' advancements have you made?"

He led us to a massive room filled with dark, sleek devices. "Cloaking. Stealth. Reconnaissance. We've made our soldiers practically invisible. We can infiltrate anywhere without detection."

Atticus whistled. "I've gotta admit, that's impressive."

Kian smirked again. "Of course it is."

Next, we headed to Phoenix Labs. The building looked like a volcano erupted and someone decided it was a good idea to build a high-tech facility inside the crater. Flames flickered from various machines, and the whole place felt like it was pulsing with fiery energy.

Akira, leader of the Phoenix faction, was there to greet us. "You ready to see what real firepower looks like?"

I nodded, even though I was half-expecting something to blow up. "Show us."

She led us to a room filled with glowing warheads. "We're combining fire magic with explosive technology. The result? Boom."

Delver blinked. "Boom?"

Akira grinned, holding up a small device. "Boom."

She pressed a button, and a tiny explosion went off in the distance, rocking the ground beneath us. "That's what we're working with."

"Okay, yeah," I said, feeling the floor tremble. "That's definitely boom."

Lastly, we made our way to Griffonworks, the Avian faction's research institute. The place was built on a high mountain, with sleek, aerodynamic structures that looked like they could take off and fly at any moment.

Inside, their focus was clear: physical enhancements. Soldiers were training with new exoskeletons, boosting their speed and strength tenfold. It was like watching an army of superheroes in the making.

Akuma tilted her head. "They're really going all out on physical enhancements."

"Of course they are," I said. "It's what they do best."

By the time we got back to Draconis Lab, my head was spinning with everything we'd seen. Every faction had its own approach, its own strengths. But one thing was clear: we were all preparing for something big.

And it wasn't just a question of if the war would come. It was when.

Back at Draconis Lab, we sat in the central meeting chamber—a round room with sleek, metallic walls and a holographic projector in the middle of the table. Everyone looked exhausted, but we knew we couldn't slow down now. The aliens hadn't even arrived yet, and we were already behind schedule.

"So," I began, leaning forward with a grin. "Any groundbreaking, galaxy-saving ideas?"

Atticus sighed dramatically. "How about we invent a machine that turns stress into energy? Because at this rate, I'll be able to power a small planet."

"Or," Delver added, "a weapon that makes people fall asleep instantly. That way, we can put the aliens to bed before they even get a chance to fight."

Akuma gave them both a look, shaking her head. "Please tell me you're joking."

"I wish I was," Delver replied, rubbing his temples. "At least it would give us a few extra hours to think up a real plan."

The room fell silent for a moment, the only sound being the soft hum of the machinery around us. We were brainstorming, but the stakes were so high that the usual playful banter felt more like a defense mechanism. Still, we needed ideas—big ones—and fast.

"All right," I said, breaking the silence. "Let's focus. We've got the best tech and magic combined in one lab. We can't waste it. What's the craziest thing we can come up with?"

Atticus pulled up a hologram of a sleek spaceship prototype. "So, I've been thinking. What if we designed a fleet of ships that can bend space and time? You know, create miniature wormholes to jump between locations instantly."

"Wormholes?" Delver raised an eyebrow. "Do you even know how that works?"

Atticus shrugged. "Not really, but it sounds cool."

I rubbed my chin, intrigued despite the absurdity. "Okay, space-bending ships. That's one idea. What else?"

Akuma leaned forward, pulling up a different hologram of a device that looked like a strange, glowing cube. "I've been thinking about communication. We need something more advanced than just regular radio signals. What if we developed a device that could tap into the alien's communication network? We could intercept their signals, maybe even disrupt their entire system."

Delver nodded slowly, eyes narrowing in thought. "That could give us a serious advantage. Imagine knowing their strategies before they even put them into action."

"But how would we hack into an alien system that's probably way more advanced than ours?" Atticus asked.

Akuma smirked. "Leave that part to me. Phoenix tech can handle it."

I couldn't help but laugh. "Of course. I'd expect nothing less from the queen of chaos herself."

The ideas started flowing from there. Once we broke the initial awkward silence, the creativity came pouring out. Some of the concepts were wild, borderline impossible, but hey, we were already mixing magic and technology—what's one more leap?

Idea #1: The Elemental Particle Cannon

Delver suddenly snapped his fingers, pulling up a new hologram. "Okay, hear me out: an Elemental Particle Cannon."

I raised an eyebrow. "What's that?"

"It's a long-range weapon that combines elemental magic with particle beams. Think of it like shooting a lightning bolt wrapped in fire and frost, but on a scale large enough to take out a spaceship."

"Sounds... a little dangerous," I said, trying to picture it.

"That's the point," Delver grinned. "We don't need to just survive this war—we need to make them fear us. Imagine the aliens seeing their flagship disintegrated by a blast of elemental chaos. It'll make them think twice about invading."

"I like it," Atticus admitted. "But can we actually build something like that?"

Delver nodded. "We can. It's a combination of Phoenix fire magic, Serpent stealth tech to hide the charge buildup, and Avian enhancements to boost the range."

I nodded slowly. "Okay, that's going on the list."

Idea #2: Dimensional Shields

Next up was Atticus. He pulled up a diagram of what looked like a standard energy shield but with a twist. "I've been working on a new defensive tech—a shield that doesn't just block attacks but displaces them into another dimension."

I blinked. "Wait, are you saying it would, like, teleport attacks?"

"Exactly," Atticus said with a grin. "We could redirect enemy fire into an alternate dimension. Not only would their attacks never hit us, but we could also send them somewhere random in the multiverse. Maybe even right back at them if we get the settings just right."

Akuma whistled. "That's ambitious. And very, very risky."

"Yeah, but it's worth the risk," Atticus countered. "If we get it working, we'd be nearly untouchable."

Delver shook his head in disbelief. "You've officially lost it, man. But I love it."

Idea #3: AI Soldiers

Akuma, always the practical one, pulled up the next concept—a blueprint for humanoid robots. "What if we built AI soldiers? Not just simple robots, but ones that can adapt to any combat situation. They'd have no fear, no hesitation, and could be programmed with our strongest combat tactics."

I frowned. "You mean replace our human soldiers?"

"No, not replace," Akuma clarified. "But back them up. Imagine sending in waves of AI soldiers to soften up the enemy. They could gather intel, weaken their defenses, and then our real fighters could come in and finish the job."

"I like it," I said. "We've got the tech to make it happen, especially with the research institutes backing us. And if the AI gets hacked?"

"We'll build firewalls so complex that even the aliens would need centuries to crack them," she replied confidently.

Idea #4: Bio-Magical Enhancements

Not wanting to be left out of the brainstorming session, I brought up my own concept. "What if we take the exoskeleton idea from the Avians and combine it with magical enhancements? We could create a system that boosts physical and magical capabilities at the same time."

Atticus nodded. "Like giving every soldier the power of a Phoenix or a Dragon?"

"Exactly," I said. "But on a more personal scale. They'd have the strength of ten men and the magical abilities of our strongest mages. We could make an army of elite warriors."

Delver's eyes lit up. "That could be game-changing. It'd make even our lower-percentage fighters as strong as the aliens."

The ideas kept coming—some more realistic than others, but each one had the potential to change the course of the war. The more we talked, the more I realized how far we'd come. A year ago, I'd barely known how to use half my abilities. Now, we were building advanced tech, creating hybrid magic-science weapons, and preparing to face an alien threat unlike anything humanity had ever seen.

And the clock was ticking.

Atticus, ever the dramatic one, leaned back in his chair with a sigh. "You know, if we pull this off, we're going to go down in history."

"Or die trying," Akuma added, only half-joking.

I glanced around the room at my friends—my team—and felt a surge of determination. This was what we were fighting for: not just survival, but the chance to prove that humanity, even in the face of overwhelming odds, could rise to the challenge.

“Well, no pressure then,” I said with a grin. “Let’s just make sure we don’t blow up the planet before the aliens get here.”

The brainstorming session ended with more ideas than I could count, and for the first time in a while, I felt like we were on the right track. Sure, the tech was insane, the risks were high, and the war still felt like a distant nightmare—but we were doing something. We were preparing.

Now, all we had to do was make sure we were ready when the real battle began.

CHAPTER THIRTEEN

First Contact, Last Chance

The tension in the air was palpable. The faint hum of the ship's engines barely masked the quiet murmurs of the crew, all too aware of the significance of this mission. We weren't just messing around with high-tech gadgets anymore. This was real—our first taste of war. And not against the big bad aliens who had sent us their smug little message from the stars, but against smaller alien planets in their system. Planets we needed to conquer if we wanted to secure enough evolution stones for our survival.

"Five planets," Atticus said, his voice low as he adjusted the settings on his wrist monitor. "Five planets we need to take down. Fast."

"No pressure," Delver muttered, scanning the view ahead from the command bridge. The stars blinked in the distance, their cold light a stark contrast to the firestorm we were about to unleash.

"I'm starting to think we bit off more than we can chew," Akuma whispered, leaning over the console. Her sharp eyes flicked across the data streams, her mind racing as fast as the calculations on-screen.

"Not an option," I said, a steely edge to my voice. "If we don't secure those evolution stones, it's game over. We've already unlocked some of our potential, but it's not enough. We need more, or we're toast when the real threat arrives."

The research institutes had confirmed that the smaller planets in the alien system hoarded large quantities of evolution stones—valuable, life-altering artifacts that boosted our abilities exponentially. The problem? Those planets weren't exactly going to hand them over with a friendly smile. No, this was war. And we had to win.

I stood at the head of the bridge, staring out at the darkness, knowing full well what awaited us. Each of these planets had its own defenses—nothing on the scale of the motherships we'd been warned about, but still formidable in their own right. And while they weren't the primary threat, they were stepping stones. Evolution stones.

Akuma flicked on the comms, her voice clear and commanding. "All factions, prepare for the planetary assault. Dragon squadron, you're leading the charge."

"That's us," I said, turning to Atticus and Delver. "Let's show them what we're made of."

Planet 1: Baelta

The first planet, Baelta, wasn't much to look at. A barren, rocky wasteland with spires of jagged stone reaching toward the heavens like skeletal fingers. But beneath its surface lay a cache of evolution stones, and we weren't leaving without them.

"Landing sequence initiated," the AI pilot announced.

Our ship descended through the planet's thin atmosphere, the turbulence shaking us like a toy in the hands of a hyperactive child. I gripped my seat, steadying myself as we touched down with a jarring thud. The hatch hissed open, and we were greeted by the hostile environment of Baelta—a cold, dead wind cutting through the heat of our engines.

"Let's move!" I shouted, and we charged out into the open, weapons at the ready.

We didn't get far before the natives made their appearance. A group of reptilian creatures, tall and muscular, with shimmering scales that reflected the dim light. They were armed with primitive but deadly energy weapons, and their eyes glowed with a feral intelligence.

"Atticus, on your left!" I yelled as one of the creatures lunged at him.

He dodged just in time, firing a blast of concentrated magic that sent the alien sprawling into the dirt. Delver, ever the showman, leapt into the air, a flaming sword materializing in his hand as he sliced through the enemies with deadly precision.

"These guys are tough," Delver said, landing next to me, slightly out of breath.

"Tough, but beatable," I replied. "We've got to keep pushing forward."

The battle was intense, but short. We took down the first wave of resistance quickly, using a combination of our evolved abilities and high-tech weaponry. By the time the dust settled, the planet was ours, and so were the evolution stones hidden in its depths.

"One down," Akuma said over the comms. "Four to go."

Planet 2: Cyren

Cyren was the opposite of Baelta. A lush jungle world teeming with life—and danger. The thick canopy overhead blocked out most of the sunlight, casting the entire planet in an eerie green glow. The locals here were fast, agile, and used the dense foliage to their advantage.

We had to fight smarter.

"Watch the trees," Atticus warned as we moved cautiously through the underbrush. "They're using the branches to hide."

"Not for long," I muttered, summoning a gust of wind that tore through the jungle, knocking the camouflaged attackers from their perches.

The battle was chaotic, with enemies darting in and out of the shadows, striking at us with poison-tipped arrows and energy blades. But we adapted quickly, using the environment against them. Delver, ever the master of fire magic, ignited the jungle in controlled bursts, driving the attackers out into the open where we could finish them off.

Cyren fell within hours, and we secured the second batch of evolution stones.

Planet 3: Selaun

Selaun was a desert world, with nothing but endless dunes stretching as far as the eye could see. The heat was unbearable, even for those of us with magical resistance, and the sandstorms made visibility near impossible.

"This place sucks," Delver grumbled, shielding his face from the wind.

"Focus," I snapped, scanning the horizon. "We've got to find their stronghold."

It took hours of trudging through the desert, but we finally located the underground facility where the Selaunites had stored their evolution stones. The fight that followed was brutal. These aliens were armored, their thick, leathery skin nearly impervious to our weapons. We had to outsmart them, using their own tunnels against them, trapping them in cave-ins and ambushes.

But in the end, Selaun was ours, and we added their evolution stones to our growing collection.

Planet 4: Othora

Othora was different. The inhabitants were more advanced, with technology that rivaled our own. This battle was more like a chess game than an all-out brawl, with each side testing the other's defenses, probing for weaknesses.

We had to be strategic, using a combination of stealth and brute force to take out their key installations. Atticus was in his element, hacking into their systems and shutting down their shields, while Akuma led a strike team to disable their weapons platforms.

It was a long, drawn-out fight, but we eventually wore them down. Othora's evolution stones were the most valuable yet, and we left the planet knowing we were one step closer to our goal.

Planet 5: Nirell

Nirell was the hardest. The atmosphere was toxic, the terrain inhospitable, and the locals were... something else entirely. These aliens were shape-shifters, able to blend in with their surroundings, making them nearly impossible to detect.

"They could be anywhere," Delver muttered, his eyes scanning the empty landscape.

"They could be anything," I corrected, my hand tightening on my weapon.

The battle on Nirell was one of paranoia. Every shadow, every movement out of the corner of our eyes, could be an enemy waiting to strike. We had to rely on our instincts, working together to flush them out and eliminate them before they could take us down.

But in the end, we did it. Nirell fell, and with it, the last of the evolution stones we needed.

We returned to Draconis Lab victorious, our ship loaded with enough evolution stones to secure the future of our people. But the weight of what we had done hung heavy over us. Five planets, five conquests. We had won, but at what cost?

"Five planets in the bag," Atticus said quietly as we stepped off the ship. "But something tells me this was just the beginning."

I nodded, my mind already racing ahead to what came next. The real war—the one we had been preparing for—was still on the horizon.

But for now, we had what we needed.

We had evolved.

Returning to Earth was a strange mix of victory and dread. The adrenaline was still pumping, but beneath it all was an undercurrent of tension that none of us could shake. We'd conquered five alien planets. Secured the evolution stones. But deep down, we all knew it wasn't enough—not nearly.

I stepped off the ship and onto the landing pad at Draconis Lab, the research institute our faction had commandeered. The sleek, metallic structure loomed over us, a shining example of the advanced technology we had at our disposal—most of it, courtesy of the angels. The air was electric, buzzing with activity as scientists and strategists ran every which way, their faces lit with excitement and worry in equal measure.

"You're back!" a voice called out from behind me. I turned to see Dr. Magnus, the lead researcher of Draconis Lab, rushing toward us. He looked exhausted, his lab coat stained and rumpled, but his eyes were wide with anticipation.

"Tell me you got them," he breathed, barely able to contain himself.

I held up a shimmering evolution stone, its surface glowing faintly in the light. "Oh, we got them," I said with a smirk.

"Five planets' worth," Delver added, walking up beside me and tossing his own stone into the air with a casual flick of his wrist.

Dr. Magnus practically vibrated with excitement. "This... this changes everything," he muttered, more to himself than to us. "With these stones, we can enhance our forces, push humanity's evolution even further..."

His voice trailed off as his eyes darted around, no doubt already thinking about the hundred experiments he was about to run.

"Yeah, yeah, that's great, Doc," I said, clapping him on the shoulder to snap him out of it. "But we need more than just stronger soldiers. We need strategy. We need ideas."

"You'll get them," he promised, looking almost delirious. "I've been in touch with the other research institutes. We've been pooling resources, working on something big."

"Something big?" Atticus stepped forward, his arms crossed, eyebrow raised. "What kind of big?"

Dr. Magnus blinked, then gave a nervous laugh. "You'll see."

The next few days passed in a blur. Draconis Lab was in full gear, and the other factions' research institutes were racing to keep up. Each faction had its own institute—Phoenix with its floating citadel of fire and ash, Avian with their sleek, metallic fortress in the mountains, Serpent's shadowy underground facility. We were all working toward the same goal, but with different focuses.

Draconis Lab was all about raw power, honing in on our combat abilities and perfecting our use of the evolution stones. Phoenix focused on aerial superiority and explosive offense, creating tech that could rain fire from the skies. Avian was developing cutting-edge armor and ground-based tech to keep their forces resilient, while Serpent specialized in stealth, espionage, and counter-intelligence.

It was like one big brainstorming session—if brainstorming involved a bunch of highly volatile materials and people who probably shouldn't be allowed near anything flammable.

"Alright, team," I said, standing at the center of the briefing room, my voice echoing slightly in the cavernous space. The giant holo-table in front of us projected the five planets we had conquered, each one marked with its own stats and resources. "We've secured the stones. Now we need to figure out how to use them to give us the best shot in the real war."

"Which means we're gonna need evolution upgrades," Delver said, spinning one of the holographic planets around with a flick of his hand. "And a lot of them."

"Already working on it," Akuma chimed in, her fingers flying across the console as she pulled up the schematics for a new piece of tech her institute was developing. "We've been testing out a hybrid system. Part magical, part physical. Something that could give us an edge in both realms."

"That's all well and good," Atticus said, leaning back in his chair, "but what about long-range intel? If the real war is coming, we're gonna need to know exactly what we're up against."

Akuma nodded. "Serpent's already on it. They're developing advanced recon drones, cloaked tech that can gather intel on the enemy without being detected. It's still in the prototype stage, but if we can get it working..."

"That's what I like to hear," I said, glancing around at the team. "So, what's the next step? We've got the stones, but how do we distribute them? Who gets them?"

"We'll need to test the limits of the stones first," Dr. Magnus spoke up from his corner of the room, looking a little less manic now. "Each stone reacts differently depending on the individual's vibrational frequency and the traits they possess. We can't just hand them out at random."

"Sounds like we're in for some fun science experiments," Delver said with a grin.

"Oh, you have no idea," Dr. Magnus muttered darkly.

Later that evening, we gathered in the main lab to start the testing. The evolution stones sat on a sleek black table, glowing softly like tiny stars. I could feel the energy radiating from them, the raw power contained within. My hand itched to grab one, to see what kind of transformation it would trigger in me.

"Alright," Dr. Magnus said, stepping up to the table. "We'll start with a basic test. Eleanor, since you're already the most evolved, I want you to take this stone and see if it triggers any further changes."

I picked up the stone, its surface warm against my palm. The moment I touched it, I felt a rush of energy surge through me. My vision blurred, and for a moment, it felt like I was floating—disconnected from everything.

Then, the changes hit.

My muscles tensed, my bones felt like they were shifting, evolving. My already heightened senses sharpened even more. I could hear the faint hum of the lab's machinery, the soft breathing of everyone around me. And then, my body... adapted.

"Uh, Doc," I said through clenched teeth. "What exactly did you give me?"

Dr. Magnus looked at the readouts on his console, his eyes widening. "Incredible," he breathed. "Your physical traits have increased exponentially. You're stronger, faster, more agile... And there's something else."

"What?" I asked, bracing myself for more bad news.

He tapped on the screen. "You've unlocked a new passive trait. Something called Chrono Reflexes. It seems to give you enhanced reaction time—almost like you're perceiving time more slowly than the rest of us."

I blinked. "So... I can dodge stuff easier?"

"Basically."

"Well, that's useful."

Atticus smirked. "Let me try."

He grabbed a stone and, almost immediately, his entire body lit up with a fiery aura. The air around him shimmered with heat, and his eyes glowed with a dangerous intensity. When the light faded, he stood there, grinning like a maniac.

"What's the verdict?" he asked, flexing his fingers as flames flickered along his skin.

Dr. Magnus checked the console again. "You've unlocked something called Infernal Mastery. Looks like your magical abilities have been boosted. Fire-based attacks, obviously, but there's more. You're resistant to heat, and your endurance has shot through the roof."

Delver and Akuma took their turns as well, both unlocking new abilities and traits that pushed their skills even further.

We were evolving.

But deep down, I knew this was only the beginning. The small victories, the powers we were unlocking—they were just stepping stones.

The real war was still out there, waiting. And we were running out of time to be ready for it.

CHAPTER FOURTEEN

That Time We Tried to Out-Science Angels

You know, there's a special kind of ridiculousness that comes with trying to outsmart beings who literally invented reality. Like, sure, we've been gifted with all this high-tech alien stuff, evolution stones, and enough power to light up the planet, but the fact that we thought we could somehow out-think the angels? Hilarious.

Especially when they were standing right next to us, watching.

"I swear this'll work," Delver muttered for the fifth time in an hour, hovering over a bunch of tech that looked more like a blender from the future. His hands moved like a mad scientist's, twisting wires, tightening screws, and, occasionally, looking way too proud of himself. "It's all about combining the right frequencies with the stones. Like—uh—well, like magic science. It's totally a thing."

"Magic science?" I raised an eyebrow, leaning against the table, casually tossing an evolution stone in the air. "You're making that up. I mean, sure, it sounds cool, but that doesn't make it real."

Delver glanced up, narrowing his eyes at me. "If you can shoot lasers out of your hands, I can create a hybrid power source with angel tech. So yes, magic science is real."

Next to us, Atticus chuckled, twirling a small flame between his fingers. "Just let him have his moment, El. He's already gone full mad scientist, and I kinda want to see what happens when he blows something up."

"Dude," Delver grumbled. "Not everything I make explodes."

"You sure about that?" Akuma smirked, pulling up a chair beside me and kicking her feet up onto the table. "Last time you built something this complicated, it nearly took out half the lab."

"That was one time."

"And we were banned from using angel tech for three weeks," I added, smirking.

Delver just huffed, focusing on his project with renewed determination. Meanwhile, the rest of us were just happy to let him keep going—mostly because it was either that, or face the prospect of actual work. Plus, if something exploded, well... bonus points for entertainment.

"So, what exactly are you trying to do this time?" I asked, watching as Delver attached some glowing crystal to a small mechanical arm.

"It's simple," he explained, as if we were all idiots for not already knowing. "I'm using the evolution stones as a power source for the tech. If I'm right, we can amplify the stones' effects. Make us stronger, faster. But only temporarily. It's like—" he paused, struggling for a comparison, "—it's like steroids for superpowers."

"Because what we really need is more superpowers," Atticus deadpanned, the flame in his hand flaring slightly. "We're already walking nukes, Del. This seems a little... excessive."

"Excessive?" Delver scoffed. "There's no such thing as excessive when you're preparing for an alien invasion."

Akuma snorted. "Says the guy who once strapped eight rockets to a hoverboard."

"That was for science!"

"Oh yeah, and it really flew," I chimed in. "Right into a wall."

Delver sighed dramatically, like we were all a bunch of unappreciative jerks. He tightened one last bolt on his gadget and stepped back, admiring his handiwork. "Okay, fine. You can mock me later. Now watch this."

He flipped a switch.

The machine hummed to life, and for a moment, everything seemed to be going smoothly. We all leaned in, curious despite ourselves. The evolution stone glowed brighter, its light pulsing in sync with the machine. It was almost... peaceful.

Then, of course, things went south.

With a loud pop and a flash of light, the entire device sparked and let out a shrill whistle. Delver yelped, jumping back as a jet of smoke erupted from the side.

"Oh, for the love of—"

"Everyone get down!" Atticus laughed, diving behind the nearest lab table like this was the most fun he'd had all week. Akuma followed suit, dragging me down with her.

Delver, still standing over his now-smoking creation, waved the fumes away like a pro. "It's fine! I just—uh—I just need to recalibrate it."

The thing gave one last, pathetic sputter before finally dying, the smoke clearing enough for us to peek out from behind our cover.

"Recalibrate," Akuma repeated, deadpan. "Right."

"Look, you're all just jealous of my genius," Delver said, clearly trying to salvage his dignity.

"Or terrified of it," I corrected, standing up and brushing off my clothes. "At this rate, you're going to invent a new kind of explosion."

Before Delver could respond, a familiar voice cut through the room.

"Still trying to out-angel the angels, I see."

I turned to see Cassiel, one of the angels overseeing the research institutes, hovering in the doorway with a knowing smirk. Her wings were folded behind her, shimmering with that irritatingly perfect, holy glow. She always looked like she had just strolled out of a painting, while we looked like lab rats who hadn't slept in days.

"We were just... experimenting," Delver said, coughing slightly from the leftover smoke.

Cassiel raised an eyebrow. "And how's that working out for you?"

"Well, nothing's on fire," I said, shrugging. "So, pretty well, I'd say."

The angel chuckled softly, stepping further into the lab. "You humans never cease to amaze me. Always pushing limits, even when you're already gifted with more power than you know what to do with."

"We're preparing," Atticus said, standing up and crossing his arms. "You heard the latest message. If we don't keep pushing ourselves, those aliens are going to wipe us out."

Cassiel's smile faded slightly. "I did hear. And believe me, we're doing everything we can to help. But don't forget—the more you rely on raw power, the more you risk losing sight of the bigger picture."

"Which is?" Delver asked, clearly skeptical.

"Strategy," Cassiel said simply. "Teamwork. Intelligence. These evolution stones are tools, but they're not the answer to everything. You'll need more than just strength to win this war."

It was quiet for a moment. We all knew she was right. As much as we joked about blowing things up and getting stronger, the reality was... we were running out of time. The war was coming, and we weren't ready.

"So, what do we do?" I asked finally.

Cassiel looked at me, her expression softening. “You keep preparing. But don’t forget what makes you human—your creativity, your adaptability. Use these gifts wisely, and you’ll stand a chance.”

“And if we don’t?” Atticus asked.

Cassiel smiled faintly. “Then I guess we’ll all find out just how powerful those evolution stones really are.”

With that, she turned and walked out of the lab, leaving us all standing in awkward silence.

“Well,” I said after a beat. “That was encouraging.”

Delver sighed, looking down at his fried machine. “I guess it’s back to the drawing board.”

Atticus slapped him on the back. “Cheer up, buddy. At least you didn’t blow anything up this time.”

“Yet,” Akuma added with a grin.

I rolled my eyes. “Let’s just hope that when the time comes, we’re not the ones getting blown up.”

And with that, we got back to work—because if we were going to survive this, we had a lot more magic science to figure out.

“So, where do we start?” Atticus asked, as we all gathered around the charred remains of Delver’s invention. He leaned on the counter, his eyes scanning the mess as if trying to divine some hidden meaning in the scorched wires.

“I’m thinking less sparks, more... I don’t know, actual functionality?” Akuma suggested, poking one of the metal pieces with a pencil. “That seems like a good first step.”

Delver was already pulling up another holographic blueprint, fingers swiping through the design as if he hadn’t just watched his last attempt go up in smoke. “It just needs a little fine-tuning. The power from the evolution stone is too unstable to run through conventional circuits. But if we can rig a regulator using the alien tech, we should be able to—”

“Make it not explode?” I interrupted.

He shot me a look. “Make it channel the power safely.”

“Safely exploding,” Atticus said, nodding wisely. “Totally a thing.”

“I’ll take ‘Not Exploding’ for a thousand, Alex,” I muttered, crossing my arms and watching as Delver’s new design started to take shape in the air.

Cassiel’s words kept echoing in my head, though. Sure, we were getting stronger, smarter. We had the tech, the evolution stones, and a ticking clock. But all the power in the world didn’t matter if we didn’t have a plan.

"What's the latest from the research institutes?" I asked, leaning over to glance at the schematic.

Each faction had their own institute now—massive facilities, half-built by human hands, half-by angelic intervention. They were like something straight out of a sci-fi movie: sleek, metallic buildings with glowing energy cores at the center, surrounded by labs filled with advanced tech and enough gadgets to make any scientist drool. If you looked at them from above, you'd think we were preparing for a mission to colonize space instead of gearing up for an alien war.

Akuma pulled up her tablet, tapping through the most recent updates. "Dragon's institute is working on weaponry enhancements, naturally. Phoenix is focusing on aerial combat tech, which—surprise, surprise—involves a lot of firepower."

"Avian's still sticking with physical augmentation," Atticus added. "They've got some crazy stuff going on with gravity control and kinetic energy absorption. Pretty sure one of their prototypes almost turned someone into a human bouncy ball."

"Classic Avian," I said, smirking. "And Serpent?"

Akuma glanced up. "Stealth tech. They're designing cloaking devices that could hide an entire battalion. Perfect for reconnaissance."

The tension in the room shifted as we all absorbed the info. For months, we'd been making progress, but suddenly it felt like it wasn't enough. Time was slipping through our fingers, and every day we inched closer to a reality none of us were ready to face. The aliens weren't just coming—they were already watching.

"What about us?" I asked, looking back at Delver's blueprints. "We've got the evolution stones, we've got all this fancy tech, but we don't have a strategy."

Akuma let out a low whistle. "Wow. You actually said the S-word."

"I mean, I hate to admit it, but... Cassiel's right," I said, rubbing the back of my neck. "We can't just throw power at the problem and hope it sticks. We need an actual plan."

"Okay, so what's the plan?" Delver asked, still tinkering with his designs but clearly listening.

I hesitated, feeling the weight of responsibility settle on my shoulders. "We test everything. Find out what works and what doesn't. We push the limits of the evolution stones, figure out how far they can take us, and then we coordinate with the other factions."

"Coordinate?" Atticus raised an eyebrow. "You do realize we've spent most of our time trying to one-up each other, right? Phoenix barely talks to us, Avian thinks we're showoffs, and Serpent—well, we don't even know where they are half the time."

"I'm aware," I said, biting back a groan. "But unless we want to get wiped off the map, we're going to have to put our egos aside and work together. At least until the aliens are dealt with."

Akuma sighed dramatically. "Wow, this really is getting serious, isn't it?"

"I know, right? Who knew saving the world would be such a drag?" I muttered, shaking my head. "But seriously, we need to get our act together. We've got some crazy alien tech, we've got magic, and we've got angels on our side. If we play this right, we might actually stand a chance."

"Assuming we don't accidentally blow ourselves up first," Atticus added, flashing a grin.

Delver rolled his eyes. "Can you please stop bringing that up?"

"Never," I said, smirking. "But seriously. Let's put our heads together and figure out how to make all this work. Starting with your magic science contraption."

Delver grinned, his eyes lighting up with excitement. "Now that's the spirit. Give me another hour and I'll have this thing running smoother than an angel's feathers."

Akuma groaned. "Please never say 'angel feathers' again."

"Fine. But when I'm the one powering up the evolution stones and saving the day, you can all thank me later."

As Delver dove back into his work, I glanced around at my team. Akuma, sarcastic as ever but always sharp. Atticus, with his unwavering confidence and infuriating good looks. Delver, the genius who sometimes forgot not everything had to explode. And me—somehow stuck leading this ragtag group of misfits, all because I had the dubious honor of being the strongest.

A part of me couldn't help but wonder if we were really up to the challenge. We'd taken down five smaller alien planets, sure. Secured enough evolution stones to keep us from crumbling under the pressure. But deep down, we all knew it was only a matter of time before the real war began.

And when it did, we'd need more than just power to survive.

We'd need each other.

And that's how we ended up working late into the night, experimenting with tech that made no sense, training with stones that could rewrite our DNA, and occasionally dodging explosions.

Because, let's be real—what's a little destruction when the fate of the world's on the line?

40

CHAPTER FIFTEEN

Surviving Science: A Guide to Not Blowing Up Your Friends

"Alright, who wants to test it this time?" Delver asked, holding up what looked like a glowing, futuristic slingshot. "I promise, this one probably won't explode."

I glanced over at Atticus, who immediately raised his hands in surrender. "Nope, not it. Last time I tested one of your gadgets, I spent three hours regrowing my eyebrows."

"You're still better off than Akuma," I said, nodding at her as she filed her nails in the corner. "She hasn't gone near anything Delver's built since 'The Fireball Incident.'"

Akuma didn't even look up. "One time. I get burned one time, and suddenly I'm the coward?"

"Your entire head was on fire," Atticus pointed out. "I think you've earned the right to be cautious."

Delver sighed, looking genuinely wounded. "You guys act like I'm some kind of mad scientist."

"You're literally a mad scientist," I said.

He threw up his hands in exasperation. "I'm trying to save the world here! Can't a guy invent without everyone bringing up past—"

"Explosions?" Atticus finished.

"Thank you for proving my point," Delver muttered.

I rolled my eyes, crossing my arms as I surveyed the wreckage of our latest brainstorming session. The Dragon Faction's research institute had officially turned into a high-tech junkyard. We had wires dangling from the ceiling, half-built machines scattered across every surface, and at least three pieces of equipment that were making ominous beeping noises. None of us dared to go near them.

"Okay," I said, stepping forward. "Let's try to focus here. We've got six months left before we're supposed to start mass-producing this stuff, and we've barely scratched the surface."

Atticus chuckled. "Yeah, because every time we scratch the surface, it blows up in our faces."

"That's not fair," Delver said defensively. "Sometimes it just sparks a little."

I sighed, rubbing my temples. "Alright, what exactly are we trying to do with... whatever that is?" I pointed at Delver's glowing slingshot, which was humming in a way that made me deeply uncomfortable.

"This," Delver said, puffing out his chest like a proud inventor, "is the Evolution Harvester 3000."

Atticus blinked. "What happened to the first 2999?"

"They were prototypes," Delver said quickly. "This is the final version."

I wasn't convinced. "And what does the 'final version' do?"

"It harvests the energy from an evolution stone and—"

"Does it explode?" Akuma interrupted, still filing her nails but clearly paying attention now.

Delver hesitated. "It... might cause a small, controlled explosion."

Atticus groaned. "There it is."

I shook my head, suppressing a laugh. "Okay, Delver, we're going to need something a little less... volatile. Remember, the point is to safely harness the evolution stones' energy, not turn us all into crispy critters."

"Hey, I'm working with what I've got!" Delver said defensively. "The energy in these stones is unlike anything we've ever seen. It's going to take time to figure out how to stabilize it."

I patted him on the back. "I believe in you, buddy. I just don't believe in your gadgets."

"Wow, thanks for the vote of confidence," Delver muttered.

"You'll live." I turned to the others. "Okay, let's take a break. We've been at this for hours, and my brain's about to explode from sheer frustration. At least, I hope it's frustration."

"Or it's one of Delver's machines," Atticus said, eyeing the slingshot.

Akuma finally stood up, stretching her arms above her head. "Honestly, a break sounds good. I need a mental reset before I get back into the 'don't die from accidental electrocution' mindset."

As we walked away from the lab, the tension lifted a little. Sure, we were in the middle of preparing for a literal alien war, but we still had to live with each other in the meantime. And part of that meant surviving Delver's death-traps-in-disguise.

We all ended up outside, sitting around a makeshift fire pit we'd built near the research facility. The night air was crisp, the stars twinkling overhead as if they had no idea the universe was on the brink of disaster. For a moment, everything was peaceful.

Atticus broke the silence. "So, what's the plan if Delver blows up the lab?"

"We move to Akuma's lab," I said, shrugging.

Akuma grinned. "Yeah, no. You blow up one more lab, and I'm instituting a 'No Delver Allowed' policy."

Delver threw up his hands. "Oh, come on! I'm not that bad."

"Uh-huh. And I'm sure those smoking ruins behind us are just part of your 'aesthetic,' right?" Atticus said.

Delver glared at him, but couldn't argue with the facts. "Fine. I'll admit... there's room for improvement."

We all laughed, but deep down, I knew we couldn't afford too many more failures. Time was running out, and the evolution stones were our best shot at leveling the playing field against the aliens. If we couldn't figure out how to use them properly, we'd be in serious trouble.

Still, I had to give Delver credit. He never gave up, no matter how many times his experiments went up in flames. And maybe, just maybe, that stubborn determination was exactly what we needed.

"Alright," I said after a long pause. "Tomorrow, we hit it hard. We've got tech to master, evolution stones to stabilize, and about a billion ways this could all go wrong. But we're not going to quit."

"Yeah," Atticus said, stretching out. "Because if we quit, we'll probably get vaporized by aliens. Motivation at its finest."

"Exactly," I said, smirking. "So, get some sleep, recharge your brains, and tomorrow, we get back to not blowing ourselves up."

"Hopefully," Akuma added.

I grinned. "Yeah. Hopefully."

And with that, we settled into the night, the fire crackling quietly as we prepared for whatever chaos the next day would bring.

Tomorrow, on "Delver's Lab of Doom": Will the Evolution Harvester 3000 finally work, or will we need to invent a new term for "catastrophic failure"? Stay tuned!

I woke up the next morning with a weird sense of foreboding. Not the "we're about to face an alien invasion" kind, but the "something absurd is going to happen" kind. With our track record, that feeling was usually right.

We gathered around Delver's latest contraption—the Evolution Harvester 3000. I still wasn't convinced it wouldn't blow us sky-high, but it was the only thing standing between us and successfully harnessing the power of evolution stones.

"Okay," Delver said, looking more confident than usual. "I made some adjustments overnight. I think—no, I know—this is going to work."

"Please define 'work,'" Akuma said, arms crossed. "Because if 'work' means 'not explode,' I'm on board."

Delver glared at her. "It's going to harvest the energy without any catastrophic incidents. I promise."

"Delver, you can't even make toast without catastrophic incidents," Atticus said, but there was a hint of excitement in his voice. Even he was curious about this.

I sighed, giving the slingshot a wary look. "Alright, let's do it. But if this blows up, I'm letting Akuma handle all future experiments."

Delver's eyes widened in horror. "Her? She'll just lock me in a corner and never let me near another tool again!"

"Exactly." I gestured at the device. "So don't mess it up."

He muttered something under his breath, but got back to work, making final adjustments to the glowing contraption. The Evolution Harvester 3000 hummed to life, the blue light pulsing steadily. We all took a step back. Just in case.

"Okay," Delver said, voice tense. "Let's see what happens."

He carefully loaded an evolution stone into the device. It slid into place with a soft click, and the glow of the stone mixed with the machine's light. The humming got louder, and we all held our breath.

For a solid five seconds, nothing happened. I almost thought it had failed—until the slingshot gave off a soft, musical chime.

"That's new," Atticus said cautiously.

"Wait for it," Delver said, grinning.

The light around the device intensified, and suddenly, a surge of energy shot out from the machine. But instead of exploding in our faces (which was a huge win for us), the energy began to swirl in the air, crackling with power. It looked like we'd captured a piece of a storm, only... prettier.

We stared, wide-eyed, as the swirling energy coalesced into a stable, glowing orb hovering above the slingshot.

"It... it worked?" I said, still half-expecting something to go wrong.

Delver was grinning like a madman. "It worked!"

We all just stood there for a moment, letting that sink in. No explosions. No fires. No emergency evacuations. Just... success.

Atticus stepped forward, cautiously poking the glowing orb. "Is it safe?"

"It's stable," Delver said confidently. "We can harness this energy and use it to supercharge our evolution process. This... this is going to change everything."

I exchanged glances with Akuma, and for once, even she looked impressed. "Alright, genius. I'm officially impressed," she said, arms uncrossing. "You didn't blow us up. Good job."

"High praise coming from you," Delver said, grinning even wider.

Atticus was still eyeing the glowing orb. "So, how exactly do we use this? Do we, like, eat it?"

"Please don't eat it," Delver said, looking horrified. "No, we can channel this energy directly into our bodies. It'll enhance our evolution traits without the need for the raw stone."

"Cool," I said, reaching toward the orb. "So what happens if—"

The moment my hand touched the orb, a jolt of power surged through me. It wasn't painful, but it was intense. My entire body felt like it was buzzing with energy, my vision going white for a split second. I stumbled back, but Atticus caught me before I could hit the ground.

"Whoa," I muttered, blinking rapidly. "That was... a lot."

Delver looked like a kid on Christmas. "What happened? Did it work? What do you feel?"

I took a deep breath, feeling the power coursing through me. It was as if every muscle, every cell in my body had been supercharged. I felt stronger, faster... more alive.

"I feel..." I started, then paused, glancing at Atticus and Akuma. "Like I could punch through a mountain."

"Please don't punch through anything," Akuma said, raising an eyebrow.

Atticus was still holding onto my arm, looking at me with a mix of concern and curiosity. "You sure you're okay? You looked like you were going to pass out for a second."

"I'm fine," I said, giving him a reassuring smile. "Better than fine, actually."

Delver was practically bouncing on his feet. "So it worked! This is it! We can use this to boost everyone's evolution traits! We'll be unstoppable!"

I wasn't sure about "unstoppable," but there was no denying that the Evolution Harvester 3000 had just given us a massive advantage. If we could refine the process and safely harness the power of evolution stones, we'd have a real shot at standing up to the alien threat.

"Okay," I said, standing up a little straighter. "So now we figure out how to replicate this for the entire faction."

Atticus grinned. "I'm assuming that means I get a turn with the orb?"

I smirked. "Go for it. Just don't pass out."

Atticus reached for the orb, and as soon as his fingers brushed it, the same surge of energy hit him. He stumbled, eyes wide, but managed to stay on his feet.

"Whoa," he said, shaking his head. "That's... that's wild."

Delver was practically vibrating with excitement. "You guys have no idea what this means! This is the breakthrough we've been waiting for!"

Akuma finally approached the orb, her expression thoughtful. "Alright, let's see what this does for me."

She reached out, her fingertips barely grazing the glowing energy. The moment they made contact, the same surge of power shot through her, but instead of stumbling back, Akuma stood tall, letting the energy flow through her like she was born for it.

She smirked. "Not bad. Not bad at all."

We all stood there, buzzing with excitement—and literal energy—realizing that this was the turning point. This was how we'd level the playing field. With the evolution stones, we could actually stand a chance in the war.

"Okay," I said, feeling the weight of the moment. "Now, let's get to work. We've got a lot of people to power up."

And so, with Delver's invention finally not blowing up in our faces (a miracle unto itself), we prepared to bring this newfound power to the rest of the Dragon faction. The war might still be a long way off, but for the first time, it felt like we actually had a shot.

Tomorrow: How many people can we evolve before something inevitably goes wrong? Stay tuned for "Evolution Madness: Don't Try This At Home!"

CHAPTER SIXTEEN

We Accidentally Create Superhumans—Oops

So, as it turns out, making people superhuman isn't all sunshine and rainbows. It's mostly chaos. Glorious, hilarious chaos.

Day one of "Operation: Let's Not Blow People Up" (my name for it, obviously) began bright and early. We gathered the entire Dragon faction around the Evolution Harvester 3000, which Delver swore was now "fully operational and 100% safe." He'd said the same thing about his homemade toaster last week, which resulted in a small kitchen fire, but hey, optimism is important.

"Alright, people!" I said, addressing the crowd of eager faces. "Today's the day we evolve! And by 'evolve,' I mean hopefully not explode, pass out, or catch fire."

Akuma raised an eyebrow from the back. "Solid motivational speech, Eleanor. Truly inspiring."

Atticus nudged me with a grin. "You should consider a career in public speaking. Maybe after we win this whole 'save the world' thing."

"Shut up and let me focus," I muttered. "This is nerve-wracking enough without your sarcasm."

Delver, standing beside the now-glowing Evolution Harvester 3000, clapped his hands together like a mad scientist about to unleash his latest experiment. Which, in this case, was pretty accurate.

"Step right up, folks!" Delver announced, clearly loving every second of this. "Who's ready to become the most powerful version of themselves?"

Silence. Nobody moved.

"Come on, guys!" I said, waving them forward. "This is literally your chance to become stronger, faster, and—dare I say—better-looking."

Still nothing. Apparently, I hadn't sold them on the "no explosions" part.

"Fine, I'll go first!" Akuma stepped forward with a dramatic sigh, pushing past a few people to reach the front. "Somebody has to prove this isn't going to end in fiery death."

Delver beamed like a proud parent. "Excellent! Step right up, Akuma. Don't be shy."

She shot him a glare but did as instructed, placing her hand on the glowing orb of energy that hovered above the machine. We all held our breath, waiting for... well, something to happen.

The air around Akuma crackled with energy as the Evolution Harvester 3000 did its thing. Her hair whipped around like she was standing in the middle of a tornado, and for a second, I thought she might actually explode—but then, just as quickly, the energy subsided.

Akuma blinked a few times, looking down at herself. "Huh," she said, flexing her fingers. "That was... intense."

"Did it work?" I asked, cautiously stepping closer.

She shrugged. "I feel stronger, I guess? Maybe a little faster. No urge to destroy things, though. Yet."

"That's probably for the best," Atticus said dryly. "We like our camp not on fire."

Delver, meanwhile, was grinning from ear to ear. "Success! The process is flawless! Akuma, you've just experienced a full evolution enhancement!"

"Great," Akuma muttered. "Do I get a T-shirt or something?"

"No T-shirts," I said, patting her on the shoulder. "But you do get bragging rights."

"Fantastic," she said, though she didn't seem too thrilled.

"Okay, who's next?" I asked, turning to the rest of the group. "It's perfectly safe! Probably!"

That didn't seem to convince anyone. In fact, most of them took a small step back. Cowards.

Atticus, of course, decided to step up next, because of course he did. "I'll do it," he said, flashing me a grin. "Can't let Akuma have all the fun."

"'Fun' is a strong word," Akuma muttered, rubbing her arm where the energy had surged through.

Atticus placed his hand on the orb with zero hesitation (because apparently he trusts Delver's inventions way more than I do), and we all watched as the same crackling energy surrounded him. For a split second, I thought his hair might catch fire (which, let's be honest, wouldn't have been a huge loss), but instead, the energy flowed through him like he'd just taken a dip in a lightning storm.

When it was over, he looked... taller? Or maybe that was just the smugness.

"Well?" I asked, raising an eyebrow. "Do you feel any different? Can you, like, lift a boulder or something?"

Atticus flexed his arm, and I swear I heard his muscles pop. "Let's just say I feel... evolved."

I rolled my eyes. "You are insufferable."

"Just jealous," he shot back, flashing me another grin.

"Okay, great," I said, clapping my hands. "Atticus didn't explode either. Everyone feel better now?"

Apparently, they did, because the line to the Evolution Harvester 3000 suddenly became a thing. One by one, people stepped up to touch the orb, and one by one, nobody exploded. Progress! And before long, our entire faction was buzzing with new energy—literally. The air around camp was crackling with it.

But, of course, nothing in life is ever simple. Especially not for us.

The problem with giving everyone in the faction a power boost is that they all get a little too enthusiastic. By the time the last person had gone through the process, half of them were running laps around the camp at breakneck speeds, and the other half were trying (and failing) to lift heavy objects to show off their new strength.

One guy—let's call him Bob—thought it'd be a great idea to challenge Atticus to an arm-wrestling match. Spoiler alert: Bob lost. Badly. He's fine, though. Probably.

Another girl tried to show off her enhanced agility by climbing a tree... and promptly fell out of said tree. She, too, is fine. Probably.

It didn't take long for chaos to descend upon the camp as everyone tested their new abilities. People were tripping over themselves, bumping into each other, and generally acting like they'd just discovered superpowers for the first time. Which, to be fair, they kind of had.

"Well," I said, watching the madness unfold. "This is... something."

"Understatement of the century," Akuma said dryly, sidestepping a guy who was running in circles at what could only be described as Mach speed.

Delver, of course, was practically glowing with pride. "This is incredible! Look at what we've accomplished! We've created a faction of superhumans!"

"Yeah," I said, watching as someone accidentally launched themselves into the air. "Superhumans who don't know how to control their powers."

Atticus chuckled beside me. "Hey, it's a learning curve. Give them a week. They'll be fine."

I shot him a skeptical look. "A week? Atticus, Bob just dislocated his shoulder trying to flex."

"Eh, small price to pay for evolution."

Akuma snorted. "If they don't knock themselves out first."

But despite the chaos, there was a strange sense of hope in the air. For the first time, it felt like we were actually ready for whatever came next. Whether that was securing more evolution stones, building up our research institutes, or, you know, preventing Bob from breaking his other arm.

"Okay, everyone!" I called out, trying to wrangle the overenthusiastic superhumans. "Maybe let's take a break before someone ends up in a full-body cast!"

As the crowd slowly (and reluctantly) began to calm down, I couldn't help but smile. Chaos aside, this was progress. We were stronger now—strong enough to face the challenges ahead. And with our new abilities, the possibilities were endless.

I just hoped we could figure out how to use them without causing too much destruction in the process.

By the next morning, the situation had escalated—and not in a good way. Apparently, giving everyone in the faction evolution stones wasn't just like giving a kid a shiny new toy. It was more like handing them a flamethrower with the instruction: “Have fun, but try not to burn down the entire camp.”

Spoiler alert: parts of the camp were now slightly on fire.

"Who let Bob near the torch?" I groaned, as smoke began to billow from one of the makeshift shelters.

"Technically, it's not Bob's fault," Akuma said, raising an eyebrow as we watched the chaos from a safe distance. "He just thinks he's fireproof."

"He's not, though."

"Nope."

"Right," I said, pinching the bridge of my nose. "Let's add 'Bob's stupidity' to the list of things we need to fix."

The problem wasn't just Bob, though. Sure, he was a big part of it, but honestly, everyone was going a little crazy. Evolution stones, it turns out, give people a serious power trip—literally. There were people running faster than sound (which, let me tell you, makes for a weird morning alarm), others flexing their newfound strength by carrying things like trees, and some had gone full ninja-mode with agility upgrades, climbing walls like they'd watched way too many superhero movies.

"How long until they get over this?" I asked, glancing at Atticus, who was lounging nearby, clearly unbothered by the insanity unfolding around us.

"Eh," he said, with a casual shrug. "Couple of days, maybe? A week tops."

"A week? Delver, by that time we won't have a camp left!"

Delver popped his head out of the nearest tent, a wrench in one hand and a weird glowing gadget in the other. "I've got solutions!" he said brightly, completely ignoring the chaos around him.

I raised an eyebrow. "Oh, this should be good."

Delver waved his weird gadget at me. "Behold! The Evolution Stone Stabilizer!"

Akuma blinked. "The what now?"

"It's supposed to stabilize all the extra energy from the evolution stones," Delver said, bouncing on his heels like a hyperactive squirrel. "Once I activate it, everyone should calm down. You know, stop setting things on fire, running through walls, all that fun stuff."

"Great," I said, crossing my arms. "And what's the catch?"

"No catch!" Delver said, looking slightly offended. "I've triple-checked it. There's like a 90% chance it'll work."

"Ninety?" Akuma asked, voice dripping with sarcasm. "That's reassuring."

"Look," Delver said, glaring at us both. "Either you trust me, or you spend the rest of the week chasing Bob and his newfound pyromania."

That... wasn't a bad point.

"Fine," I sighed. "Go for it. What's the worst that could happen?"

As soon as the words left my mouth, I regretted them. Because honestly? In this camp, saying "What's the worst that could happen?" was basically an invitation for something to go wrong.

Delver didn't seem worried, though. He activated the Stabilizer, which made a low humming noise and emitted a soft, blue glow. At first, nothing happened. I mean, nothing exploded, so that was a win. The air around camp just... shifted. I could feel it, like a weight lifting off our shoulders. The tension in the air faded.

And slowly but surely, the chaos began to subside.

One by one, people started slowing down. The guy who had been sprinting laps stopped, hands on his knees, panting like he'd just run a marathon. The group trying to build a weird stone monument (because why not?) all looked around, blinking like they'd just woken up from a dream.

"Did it work?" Akuma asked, glancing around.

"Looks like it," I said, cautiously optimistic.

Bob, covered in soot but otherwise unharmed, wandered over to us, looking slightly sheepish. "So, uh... sorry about the fire."

"Don't worry about it," I said, patting him on the back. "You'll live. Probably."

Delver, for his part, was practically glowing with pride. "I told you! Stabilizer works like a charm!"

"Good job, Delver," Atticus said, sounding genuinely impressed. "I didn't even hear any explosions this time."

"High praise," I added, giving Delver a nod of approval.

For once, everything seemed to be under control. Well, relatively under control. Which was about as good as things got around here. The camp was still standing, nobody was on fire, and the people had stopped acting like over-caffeinated squirrels on a sugar high.

"So," I said, addressing the group of now somewhat-reasonable people. "Now that you're all done with your superhero auditions, maybe we can focus on what's next?"

"Which is?" Bob asked, still brushing soot off his shoulders.

"Training," I said. "And figuring out how to use these powers without, you know, setting the world on fire."

"Or each other," Akuma added, shooting a glance at Bob.

"Training sounds fun," Atticus said with a grin. "I've always wanted to see how far I can throw a boulder."

"I meant organized training," I said quickly, before he got any ideas. "Like, actual combat strategies. How to use our new abilities in real fights."

"Sounds boring," Atticus muttered.

"Necessary," I corrected. "Especially now that we've gotten word from Command about securing those evolution stones on other planets."

The group quieted down at that. This was the next big step. We'd been evolving, growing stronger, but now we had to prove we could handle it—and secure more of these evolution stones for the next phase of the fight.

"The smaller alien planets should be easy enough," Akuma said. "But we'll need to be smart about it. We're powerful, but we're not invincible."

"Speak for yourself," Atticus said with a wink, but there was a seriousness behind his usual bravado. He knew just as well as the rest of us that this was no game. The stakes were rising, and the real challenge was still ahead of us.

I took a deep breath, feeling the weight of the task ahead. "Alright, let's get to work. Time to show the universe what humanity can do."

And with that, we dove headfirst into our next mission: conquering alien planets for evolution stones, one step closer to preparing for the war that loomed on the horizon.

CHAPTER SEVENTEEN

Who Knew Stealing from Aliens Could Be This Fun?

You know what's more nerve-wracking than stealing from aliens? Doing it with a guy who still thinks fireproof and "probably fireproof" are the same thing. Yep. Bob was with us on this mission.

"Alright," I whispered, as we crouched behind a rock formation on Planet #1 (which we named 'Rocktopia' for the endless sea of boulders). "Everyone knows the plan, right?"

"Get in, grab the evolution stones, don't die," Atticus said, his face showing exactly zero concern. He seemed more interested in a pebble he was tossing up and down. "Simple."

"Yeah, no," I said, glaring at him. "There's more to it than that. You have to take out the sentries quietly, Delver needs to disable their defense system, and Akuma and I will—"

"Destroy everything," Bob interjected, his eyes shining with excitement.

"No, Bob," Akuma sighed. "We are not blowing up the alien base."

He looked mildly disappointed.

The truth was, we'd done okay with the last few missions. Securing evolution stones from smaller planets had been more like... intergalactic scavenger hunts than actual combat. But this time? This time, we were dealing with a fully-manned alien outpost. These guys knew we were coming—or at least, they were prepared for something.

"Remember," I continued, trying to keep the group focused. "We don't need to fight unless we have to. Just get in, get the stones, and get out."

"I still vote for blowing up the base," Bob muttered under his breath.

Atticus grinned. "That's the spirit."

"Look," I said, before this conversation got even further off-track, "the last thing we need is for this to turn into a full-blown firefight with the aliens. We're trying to keep a low profile, remember?"

"Low profile?" Delver asked, glancing at my glowing white hair. "Right."

"Details," I said, waving him off. "Let's move."

Crawling across the jagged surface of Rocktopia was not how I envisioned intergalactic missions going. But, here we were, crawling like crabs while trying to avoid alien detection. We finally reached the edge of the base—an ugly, metal monstrosity that looked like someone had built it out of a LEGO set designed by an architect on way too much coffee.

Atticus, being the stealth expert of our group, was first to move. He slinked forward with all the grace of a ninja cat, disappearing into the shadows. We watched as he took out the two sentries guarding the entrance with barely a sound. A flash of steel, a quiet thud, and they were down. He gave us a thumbs-up.

"Show-off," Akuma muttered, but there was a smile on her face.

"Delver, you're up," I said, nudging him forward.

Delver had the unenviable job of hacking into their defense system. Because, you know, every alien base has one of those. We were trying not to think about what might happen if he didn't succeed. No pressure or anything.

He quickly slipped over to the control panel, his fingers flying across the alien interface like a mad scientist. "Just a few more... and... got it!" he whispered, as the base's lights dimmed.

"Nicely done," I said, feeling a little more hopeful. "Now, let's—"

Suddenly, there was a loud crash from behind us. I whipped around, my heart sinking.

Bob.

"Sorry!" Bob hissed, struggling to get up after knocking over what looked like an entire pile of alien tech.

I covered my face with my hand. "Of course."

"We're good, we're good!" Bob whispered, waving his arms like that would somehow make everything better. "Nothing's broken!"

"Except our cover," Akuma muttered.

Before we could properly chew Bob out, there was a loud clanking sound—the unmistakable sound of alien footsteps approaching.

"Okay, change of plans!" I said, standing up and drawing my sword. "Prepare to—"

"Destroy everything?" Bob said, his eyes lighting up again.

"Fight!" I corrected, though by now, destruction was a given.

The first wave of alien guards rounded the corner, and we went straight into battle mode. Akuma summoned flames, her hands crackling with energy as she launched a barrage of fireballs at the incoming guards. Atticus took the stealthy approach, using his agility to leap from one alien to the next, knocking them out cold before they even realized what hit them.

I, of course, had my own hands full. A massive, blue-skinned alien charged at me with what looked like a club made out of a space rock. I blocked the blow with my sword, the impact sending a shockwave up my arm. But instead of backing down, I smirked and spun around, slashing at his legs. He went down with a grunt.

"Delver, get those stones while we hold them off!" I shouted.

"I'm on it!" he yelled back, already sprinting toward the chamber where the evolution stones were stored.

By now, the base was in full chaos. Sirens blared, aliens swarmed from every direction, and Bob—well, Bob was laughing maniacally as he blasted through enemy ranks with a stolen plasma cannon.

"Why do we keep bringing him?" Akuma shouted over the noise, dodging a laser shot from a nearby alien.

"Because he's weirdly effective!" Atticus shouted back, flipping over an alien guard and delivering a swift punch to its face.

Delver finally returned, a glowing box clutched in his hands. "Got the stones! Let's get out of here before they call in reinforcements!"

"About time," I muttered, as we started making our escape. We fought our way back to the entrance, with Bob covering us by... causing as much mayhem as possible. By the time we reached the exit, half the base was on fire, but hey—mission accomplished.

"Everyone ready?" I asked, glancing at the group as we prepared to warp back to our ship.

"Just another day in paradise," Atticus said with a grin, tossing his pebble in the air.

"Let's never come back here," Akuma groaned, wiping the soot off her face.

"Agreed," I said, as we activated the warp drive, leaving Rocktopia—and the flaming alien base—behind us.

As soon as we were back on the ship, I let out a sigh of relief and slumped against the nearest wall. "Well, that went... exactly as expected."

"At least we got the stones," Delver said, holding up the box with a proud grin.

Bob, still clutching his plasma cannon, beamed at us. “And I didn’t even blow up the entire base!”

“Small victories,” I muttered. “Small victories.”

Akuma sighed, rolling her eyes. “Next time, we need a better plan.”

Atticus chuckled. “Next time? Please. This was perfect. Who knew stealing from aliens could be this fun?”

When in Doubt, Blame Bob

The return trip to Earth wasn't exactly a smooth one. Our ship, the Vigilant Horizon, jerked and rattled like a kid shaking a snow globe. Apparently, intergalactic travel isn't immune to turbulence. Who knew?

Atticus lounged in one of the cockpit seats, hands behind his head, looking as if we weren't plummeting through space at warp speed. "So, how many alien planets are left on the hit list?"

I glanced at the mission log, which Delver had somehow managed to update while the ship shuddered like it was trying to break apart. "Five down, three to go. That's assuming we don't get incinerated by a stray meteor."

"Sounds like a fun week ahead," Atticus said, yawning.

Delver rolled his eyes from the console. "Can we at least pretend this is serious? We just stole evolution stones from a planet that wasn't exactly thrilled to have us."

"Oh, they loved us," Atticus grinned. "I could tell by the way they tried to fry us with plasma bolts."

Akuma, sitting cross-legged near the ship's rear, was twirling a small flame between her fingers. She looked up, eyes narrowing at Atticus. "We wouldn't have had to dodge plasma bolts if someone hadn't decided to knock over an entire pile of alien tech."

All eyes turned to Bob, who was currently balancing the plasma cannon on his lap, looking way too proud of himself.

"What?" Bob asked, completely clueless. "I said I was sorry."

"Sorry doesn't fix the fact that you set off an alarm and almost blew up the ship's engine," I said, crossing my arms. "Next time, maybe leave the alien tech alone."

Bob just shrugged. “Hey, the cannon works, doesn’t it?”

“Great, we can add ‘armed with stolen alien weaponry’ to our growing list of galactic crimes,” Delver muttered.

Before I could add anything to the Bob-reprimanding, the ship’s communication system crackled to life. “Incoming message from Earth command,” the robotic voice announced.

I sighed and activated the holo-screen. “This should be good.”

A familiar face appeared on the screen: Commander Oren, leader of Earth’s official defense initiative. You’d think he’d be more grateful considering we were essentially humanity’s best shot at survival, but Oren had the personality of a drill sergeant who’d been deprived of coffee for about twenty years.

“Vigilant Horizon, what’s the status on your mission?” Oren barked.

“Successful,” I replied, keeping it short. “We have the evolution stones from Rocktopia.”

Oren’s expression didn’t change. “Good. But don’t get too comfortable. We’ve received reports of alien skirmishes on the edge of the Milky Way. Seems like the smaller planets are starting to get spooked by your little... expeditions.”

I raised an eyebrow. “Skirmishes? So the aliens are starting to notice?”

“Not just notice,” Oren said, leaning closer to the camera. “They’re organizing. You’ve poked the hornet’s nest, and now the hornets are gathering.”

“Well, that’s not ominous at all,” Delver whispered, glancing at the rest of us.

“We’ll keep that in mind,” I said, not bothering to hide my sarcasm. “Anything else?”

Oren's eyes narrowed. "Yeah. Try not to blow up the next alien base. I'd like to avoid an intergalactic war until we're actually ready for one."

"Hey, that wasn't us," I said quickly. "That was all Bob."

Bob waved from the back. "Sorry, Commander!"

Oren's face twitched like he was reconsidering his career choices. "Just... don't make things worse." The screen blinked off before I could respond.

"Well," Atticus said, stretching in his seat. "That went well."

I groaned. "We're walking on thin ice here, guys. We've got more alien planets to hit, and now they're actually starting to fight back. If we mess up again, this whole evolution stone plan could backfire."

"So what's new?" Akuma said, her flames dissipating. "We've been pushing our luck since day one."

"She's not wrong," Delver muttered, checking the ship's coordinates. "We've had at least five near-death experiences just this week."

"Near-death experiences make us stronger," Atticus chimed in, always the optimist.

"Or they kill us," I countered. "Whichever comes first."

Bob finally spoke up. "At least we're still alive. And hey, we've got evolution stones! That's gotta count for something, right?"

"Yeah," I said, rubbing my temples. "But if we want to survive this thing, we need more than just stones. We need—"

Suddenly, the ship jolted violently, sending us all flying out of our seats. Lights flickered, alarms blared, and I knew in that moment: things were about to get a whole lot worse.

"Uh, what just happened?" Atticus asked, picking himself up from the floor.

Delver's fingers flew across the control panel, trying to stabilize the ship. "Looks like... we've got company."

I looked at the monitor, where a series of red blips appeared on the radar. More alien ships. Great.

"Commander Oren's gonna love this," I muttered, drawing my sword. "Everyone, get ready for round two."

CHAPTER EIGHTEEN

Aliens in the Rearview Mirror, and They're Closer Than They Appear

If you've never had an alien warship chase you through deep space, let me tell you—there's a reason why that isn't part of the official Earth Defense curriculum. It's chaotic, terrifying, and there's absolutely no way to look cool while it's happening.

"Brace yourselves!" Delver shouted over the sound of alarms, yanking the ship into a hard turn. The Vigilant Horizon groaned in protest, like a ship that just remembered it hadn't been built for this kind of abuse. "I think we've got at least three on our tail!"

"Make that four!" Akuma yelled from her station. She slammed a button that deployed our pathetic excuse for a defense mechanism—basically, space confetti meant to throw off enemy targeting systems. "And they don't seem to be in the mood for a fireworks show!"

I was strapped into the co-pilot's seat, frantically trying to get the ship's shields to regenerate. Spoiler alert: they weren't. "Shields are at twenty percent and dropping! We can't take much more of this!"

Atticus, of course, was having the time of his life. He leaned over the back of my chair, a grin plastered on his face. "Why do they always chase us? I feel like we're the universe's favorite punching bag."

"It's because of your magnetic personality," I snapped, glaring at him.

"I can't help it if I'm irresistible," he said with a wink. I considered throwing him out of the airlock, but that would take too much effort.

Bob, bless his oblivious soul, was seated behind us, somehow managing to look entirely too calm for the situation. "So... what's the plan?"

"We're working on it!" I shouted as a blast from one of the alien ships rocked the Vigilant Horizon. The lights flickered again, and I was starting to wonder if we'd make it out of this in one piece.

"We need to lose them!" Delver growled, hands flying over the controls. "I can't keep this up forever!"

Akuma's voice came through the comm system. "I can try to channel more power to the engines, but that means the shields will go down even faster."

"Well, if we get hit again, we won't have to worry about shields!" I shot back. "Do it!"

Another explosion rattled the ship, this one much closer than I liked. I could hear the hull groaning, and it made my stomach lurch. This ship had been through enough, and now it was about to become scrap metal.

Bob leaned forward, completely unaffected by the chaos around him. "Have we tried asking them to stop?"

Atticus snorted. "Yeah, Bob, why don't you send a polite memo? 'Dear Aliens, please stop shooting at us. Sincerely, the doomed humans.'"

"Hey, it might work," Bob said with a shrug.

"It won't," Delver and I said in unison.

Just as I was about to suggest a last-minute escape plan that involved screaming and hoping for a miracle, the ship's sensors picked up something ahead. A huge, floating chunk of debris, big enough to hide behind. Maybe the universe wasn't entirely out to kill us.

"There!" I pointed toward the screen. "Can we use that to shake them?"

Delver's eyes lit up. "If I time it right... hold on!"

The ship dipped and veered toward the debris, engines straining as we pushed every bit of power into our escape. The alien ships behind us kept firing, their shots barely missing as Delver twisted and turned the Vigilant Horizon like we were in some sort of interstellar dance-off. I had to give it to him—he was good at this.

As we approached the debris, Delver pulled the ship into a hard dive. The alien ships followed, too close to avoid it in time. A few of their blasts hit the floating mass, causing it to explode into a cloud of shrapnel.

"Now!" Delver yelled, pulling the ship up sharply.

We rocketed upward, leaving the alien ships to deal with the mess of debris. They didn't fare so well. The radar showed them scrambling to recover, but the explosion had done enough damage to give us the opening we needed.

"We're clear!" I breathed, slumping back in my seat. "Nice flying, Delver."

"Don't thank me yet," Delver said, his hands still gripping the controls. "We've got another problem."

I looked at him, confused. "What do you mean?"

He motioned to the console, where a new alert was flashing. "Incoming transmission. It's from one of the research institutes."

"Which one?" Akuma's voice came over the comm.

"The Phoenix Institute," Delver replied grimly.

Great. That's exactly what we needed—more problems. I patched the transmission through, and a familiar face popped up on the holo-screen. It was Professor Rhys, head of the Phoenix faction's research division. And he did not look happy.

"Eleanor," he said, his voice clipped and to the point. "We have a situation."

"Join the club," I muttered under my breath. "What's going on?"

Rhys adjusted his glasses, looking as frazzled as I'd ever seen him. "We've detected unusual energy readings coming from deep space. Something's heading toward us, and it's not friendly."

"Unusual energy readings?" Atticus asked, leaning over my shoulder. "That sounds like alien tech to me."

"Exactly," Rhys said. "But it's not just any alien tech. This is something different. Bigger. Stronger. And it's heading straight for Earth."

I felt a chill run down my spine. "How long do we have?"

Rhys frowned. "Not long. We estimate it'll reach us within the next 72 hours. And we're not prepared for this kind of attack."

"Perfect," I muttered. "Because we've been doing such a great job keeping up so far."

Rhys shot me a look. "I'm serious, Eleanor. We need all the help we can get. The Phoenix Institute is working around the clock to develop new weapons, but we need more time. If you've got any tricks up your sleeve, now's the time to use them."

I exchanged a glance with Delver and Atticus. The mood in the ship shifted from chaotic panic to something much more serious. This wasn't just another small skirmish. This was the beginning of something much worse.

"Understood," I said, my voice firm. "We'll be there as soon as we can."

Rhys nodded. "Good luck. We're all counting on you."

The transmission cut out, leaving the cockpit in tense silence. I turned to Delver. "Get us to the Phoenix Institute. Now."

He nodded, already plotting the course. "On it."

Atticus cracked his knuckles, a determined look in his eyes. "Looks like things are about to get interesting."

I sighed, feeling the weight of everything pressing down on me. "Yeah. Let's just hope we survive long enough to find out how interesting."

We had exactly three minutes to prepare before the most intense brainstorming session of my life began. The Phoenix Institute wasn't messing around. As soon as we stepped inside, we were ushered through a maze of corridors that smelled like burnt circuits and freshly printed reports. Apparently, science always smells the same, whether it's the 21st century or a thousand years into an alien war prep plan.

"Welcome to the Phoenix Institute," said Rhys, our old friend from the holo-transmission. His voice was serious, but his eyes darted between us like he was sizing up his next experiment. "We have much to discuss, and not much time to do it."

Delver looked around at the sterile walls and humming tech, visibly impressed. "I've never seen so much cutting-edge gear in one place. You guys must be printing money down here."

"Printing it and burning it at the same time," Rhys said dryly, leading us into a large conference room. The walls were covered in holographic displays, each one scrolling through endless streams of data that made my head spin.

I couldn't help but smirk. "So, what are we thinking? Giant space lasers? Anti-alien drones? Maybe a giant mech suit I can pilot?"

Rhys didn't even blink at my sarcasm. "Actually, we're thinking about all of that—and more."

Okay, so maybe the Phoenix Institute was cooler than I gave it credit for.

We took our seats around the table, and I could feel the weight of the situation settling in. There were charts, graphs, and about a million things I didn't understand flashing on the screens. This was it—the point where humans decided whether or not they'd survive.

Rhys wasted no time. "First things first: we've identified the energy signatures from the incoming alien ship. It's bigger than anything we've encountered, and it's using technology that's far more advanced than even our current estimates."

"Great," Atticus muttered under his breath. "Because we were just doing so well with the old aliens."

I elbowed him, but Rhys seemed unfazed. "We've been working with all four research institutes—Phoenix, Dragon, Avian, and Serpent—on developing new ways to counter this threat. Each faction has been focusing on a different aspect of the war effort."

He flicked his fingers, and the holograms changed, showing four massive structures—one for each faction. They looked like something out of a sci-fi movie: sleek towers brimming with alien-hybrid technology, surrounded by sprawling campuses that seemed to defy the laws of physics.

"The Phoenix Institute," Rhys continued, "has been focused on energy manipulation. Specifically, harnessing the power of the sun to create devastating weapons." He paused for effect, and I could practically hear Atticus's eyes light up with excitement. "We're working on solar-based weaponry that can vaporize enemy ships before they even reach Earth."

"Well, that's definitely on-brand," I said, nodding. "But what about the other factions? What are they up to?"

Rhys waved his hand again, and the next institute flashed on the screen.

"The Dragon Institute," he said, "is focused on developing new biological enhancements. They've been working on ways to enhance human DNA with alien genes, giving us the physical and mental capabilities needed to fight on equal footing."

Delver raised an eyebrow. "So... like, super soldiers?"

"Exactly," Rhys confirmed. "Think enhanced strength, reflexes, and the ability to withstand extreme conditions. But we're still in the early stages of testing."

Atticus leaned back in his chair, arms crossed. "Okay, so Phoenix is the big guns, and Dragon's playing Captain America. What about Avian and Serpent?"

Rhys swiped to the next screen. "The Avian Institute is focused on aerial and reconnaissance technologies. They're developing stealth drones, enhanced radar, and long-range communication systems to help us track and outmaneuver the enemy."

"And Serpent?" I asked, already sensing where this was going.

"The Serpent Institute specializes in espionage and intelligence gathering," Rhys said. "They've been working on infiltration techniques, using cloaking technology to gather data from enemy ships without being detected."

I let out a low whistle. "That's... a lot."

"And we're going to need all of it," Rhys said, looking directly at me. "We have three days before the alien ship reaches Earth, and if we're not ready by then, everything we've built so far will be for nothing."

Delver frowned. "So, we've got the tech, but how do we deploy it? We don't exactly have a space army just waiting to go."

"We've been developing ways to distribute these technologies to the general population," Rhys explained. "The biggest hurdle is getting people evolved fast enough to use them. Right now, evolution stones are the key. But there aren't enough to go around."

Akuma, who had been silent up until now, finally spoke. "So... we need more stones. A lot more."

Rhys nodded. "Precisely. And that's where the war with smaller alien planets comes in."

I sat up straight. "Wait, you're suggesting we raid other alien planets to steal their evolution stones?"

"Not just suggesting it," Rhys said, a grim smile on his face. "We've already started. Our scouts have identified five nearby planets with abundant evolution resources. If we can secure those, we'll have enough stones to evolve the entire human population."

Atticus grinned. "Space raids? I'm in."

"Hold on," I said, holding up my hand. "Let me get this straight. We're about to start a mini war with a bunch of smaller alien planets, just so we can evolve ourselves into superhumans in time for the real war?"

"Pretty much," Rhys confirmed.

I leaned back in my chair, shaking my head. "This just keeps getting crazier."

Delver crossed his arms, a serious expression on his face. "But it's our only shot. We have to do this."

Akuma nodded in agreement. "The evolution stones are our best chance at survival. If we don't act now, we won't stand a chance against the bigger threats."

I sighed, already feeling the weight of what was coming. "Alright then. Let's go steal some stones."

Rhys gave a curt nod, clearly pleased with our resolve. "You'll have all the resources you need. The ships are prepped and ready for departure. We'll brief you on the specifics before the mission begins."

As we stood to leave, I couldn't help but glance at the massive hologram of the approaching alien ship, looming like a storm on the horizon.

It was getting closer.

And we were running out of time.

CHAPTER NINETEEN

Invention Convention (Chaos Included)

When you think about it, chaos is basically just order waiting to happen—except in our case, it was more like a tornado doing the cha-cha in a crowded room. The Phoenix Institute was buzzing with activity as our team prepared for the upcoming raid on those alien planets. Scientists scurried around, throwing out ideas like they were confetti at a New Year's party, and I could practically feel the electric tension in the air.

"Okay, team!" Rhys clapped his hands, drawing our attention. "We're about to enter the most critical phase of our mission: the invention showcase! Each faction has been working on something special, and we need to figure out which innovations will be our game-changers in the field."

"Can we start with mine?" I asked, bouncing slightly in my seat. "I have a fabulous idea that combines the best elements of pizza and space travel."

Atticus chuckled. "Let me guess, a pizza launcher? Because I'm totally on board with that."

"No, no! More like a Portable Intergalactic Cuisine Dispenser! You know, for all those late-night raids when you get hungry?" I replied, waving my hands for emphasis. "It would dispense pizza-flavored fuel cells! Think about it! We'll be fueled by cheese!"

"Fuel cells powered by cheese?" Akuma said, raising an eyebrow. "Eleanor, I love pizza as much as the next person, but I don't think that's how physics works."

"Physics is just a suggestion!" I shot back, determined. "Imagine the aliens' faces when we land, covered in melted cheese. They'll be so distracted they won't know what hit them!"

"Or they'll just laugh at us," Delver pointed out, smirking.

"I like her idea," Atticus chimed in, his eyes gleaming. "But I think we should go with my Multidimensional Scavenger Drone instead. It's a small, flying device that can sneak around and collect intel—or, in your case, leftover pizza—without anyone noticing."

"Great, because I want our tactical plans to be scuttled by a cheesy drone," I said dryly, but I couldn't help but laugh.

Just as I was about to continue my pitch, a commotion erupted at the back of the room. A scientist in a lab coat stumbled forward, clutching a strange-looking device that resembled a blender fused with a fog machine.

"Uh, guys?" he called, his voice shaking slightly. "I think I might have made a little... miscalculation."

He pressed a button on the device, and suddenly the room filled with an obnoxiously bright blue mist that smelled faintly of burnt toast.

"Is this supposed to happen?" I asked, trying to wave the mist away. "Because I'm pretty sure toast is not on the approved list of alien distractions."

"Actually, it's supposed to create an invisibility field," the scientist stammered, his eyes wide. "But it looks like it's only made us smell bad!"

Everyone began to cough and splutter as the mist thickened.

"Not the best first impression to make on aliens," Akuma said, covering her nose. "Can't we just stick to the cheesy drones?"

"Okay, that's it!" Rhys shouted, waving his arms to clear the mist. "We need to regroup and focus. Time for some actual brainstorming, not mist-creating!"

As if on cue, a small group of scientists raced in, each wielding odd contraptions. One held a large, clock-like device that had too many knobs, while another had a helmet that looked suspiciously like a salad bowl.

"What's that?" Delver asked, pointing at the salad bowl helmet.

"It's the Mind-Meld Enhancer," the scientist explained, looking rather proud. "It allows users to sync their thoughts with others in the room!"

"Fantastic," Atticus said, trying to contain his laughter. "Now we can all have bad ideas at the same time!"

With the chaos swirling around us, I suddenly had an epiphany. "Wait! What if we combine the Invisibility Field with the Mind-Meld Enhancer? We could all be invisible, then meld our thoughts while raiding the alien planets!"

"Uh, Eleanor?" Akuma said, her eyes narrowing. "Are you sure that's a good idea? The last time we melded our thoughts, I think we ended up deciding to launch a pizza raid."

"Exactly!" I exclaimed, realizing I'd been accidentally promoting my pizza plan. "We'll distract them with something ridiculous while we gather evolution stones! And who wouldn't want a pizza after a long day of alien fighting?"

Rhys pinched the bridge of his nose. "That's the spirit, Eleanor. But let's try not to burn any more toast while we're at it."

"Are we seriously discussing burning toast as a strategy?" Delver shook his head, chuckling. "This mission just keeps getting better and better."

As we continued to brainstorm, the atmosphere shifted from chaotic to productive. Ideas flowed like pizza sauce—sticky and messy, but oddly satisfying. I felt a sense of camaraderie building among us, and I knew we were about to face the biggest adventure of our lives, armed with nothing more than crazy inventions and an unhealthy amount of laughter.

After all, if we were going to save the world, we might as well do it with a little cheese on the side.

The brainstorming session continued as we tossed around ideas like they were those rubber stress balls you get at conventions—bouncy, ridiculous, and more than a little useless. Rhys glanced at the smoky mess surrounding us and sighed. "Okay, back to the drawing board! What's next?"

"Let's take a step back," Akuma suggested, pulling out a notepad filled with scribbles that could only be described as "inspired." "We need to focus on our actual needs. We're heading into battle soon, and we need more than just pizza-related distractions."

"True," Atticus nodded, "but what if we could distract them with our own ridiculousness? Like, I don't know, some kind of holographic projection that makes us look like dancing chickens?"

"Why would we want to look like dancing chickens?" Delver asked, crossing his arms, a bemused expression on his face. "That sounds like a one-way ticket to getting abducted again."

"Because," I chimed in, "who would take us seriously if we're dancing? We'd look so stupid that they'd let their guard down, and then—bam! We sweep in for the evolution stones!"

"Or," Akuma interjected, "we could go with something actually useful, like a portable energy shield that can absorb alien attacks."

"Oh, that's great, Akuma," I said, waving my hands. "But where's the fun in that? Besides, have you ever tried to dance in an energy shield? It's like trying to do the cha-cha in a giant bubble!"

Just as we were deep into the chaos of our ideas, a familiar figure barged into the room. It was Kai, looking flustered and holding a small device that emitted faint sparks.

"Guys! You won't believe what I just found!" he exclaimed, his hair standing on end as if he'd just been struck by lightning. "It's a prototype for a Neuro-Linguistic Paralyzer! We can use it to freeze our enemies in place, but..."

"But what?" I asked, leaning forward, intrigued.

"But," he said, looking sheepish, "I accidentally activated it while testing it on myself. So I'm a little bit... frozen... right now."

"Great! So you're saying you can't move?" Delver grinned, trying not to laugh.

"Exactly," Kai replied, his expression a mix of annoyance and resignation. "I mean, I can blink, but that's about it."

"Can we get that to work on aliens?" Atticus asked, eyes lighting up. "Because if we can freeze them mid-laser-blast, that would be amazing!"

"Unless they just blast us while frozen!" Kai pointed out, a hint of panic in his voice.

"Relax, it's a work in progress!" I said, attempting to sound reassuring. "But I like the concept. If we can figure out how to use it effectively, we could turn the tide in our favor."

Suddenly, the inventor from before returned, looking even more frantic than before. "Um, guys! About the invisibility field—there's been a small mishap!"

"What kind of mishap?" I asked, my heart sinking.

"Well, I might have left it running for too long, and now the lab is completely invisible," he said, scratching his head. "I can't even see where I'm standing!"

"Okay, great. So now we're not only drowning in chaos, but we're also in an invisible lab?" Akuma said, incredulous. "Is that what you're telling us?"

"Exactly! But it's also kind of a blessing in disguise!" he added quickly, holding up a hand. "We can practice moving around without being detected! Just... you know... try not to bump into anything."

"Right," I said, still trying to process everything. "So we can perfect our moves while we're invisible? That's actually brilliant! Like a ninja training camp!"

"More like a ninja training camp where no one knows where anyone is!" Akuma quipped, rolling her eyes.

Just then, a loud crash echoed through the lab as someone—who shall remain nameless—tripped over a barrel of transformation juice that had been carelessly left out. The sound reverberated like a trumpet announcing our arrival at the Alien Fail Convention.

"Uh, I think we're drawing attention," Atticus muttered, peering into the invisible void. "If there are any aliens nearby, I think they're about to become very aware of our shenanigans."

"Time to put our plans into action!" I declared, adrenaline surging through me. "Let's use the chaos to our advantage!"

"Sounds like a plan," Delver said, smirking. "But first, we should probably find a way out of this invisible trap before we make any further messes."

With that, we set off into the invisible labyrinth, bumping into each other and swatting at the air as we navigated our way through the chaos. It was like an absurd game of tag, but the stakes were higher, and the alien threat loomed large.

We may not have had all the answers, but at least we had each other, a few ridiculous inventions, and an abundance of laughter. And when it came to facing an intergalactic war, that was more than enough to get us started.

CHAPTER TWENTY

The Wacky Weaponry Workshop

The invisible lab was starting to feel like a chaotic carnival—minus the cotton candy and clowns. We were knee-deep in our latest attempt to create a weapon that wouldn't blow us up before it took out the aliens. Trust me, that's a delicate balance.

"Okay, folks," I announced, gathering everyone's attention. "Today, we're going to invent something truly groundbreaking. Something that'll strike fear into the hearts of our enemies. Or at least mildly confuse them."

"Sounds like every plan we've had so far," Atticus replied with a grin, leaning against an invisible wall like a chill superhero waiting for a cue.

"Look, if we can't scare them, we can at least make them laugh," I said, flicking through my notes. "I mean, who doesn't get a chuckle out of someone slipping on a banana peel? Imagine if that banana peel could explode!"

"Oooh! I love a good banana peel idea!" Akuma clapped her hands, her eyes sparkling with mischief. "But can we make it a bit more explosive? You know, to really drive the point home?"

"Explosive banana peels, got it," I said, jotting that down. "Maybe we can sprinkle in some glitter for effect? Like, 'Surprise! You've been ambushed by an art project!'"

Kai, still stuck in his frozen state, blinked at me with exaggerated seriousness. "Just so we're clear, we're not seriously going with exploding glitter bananas, right? Because that sounds like a lawsuit waiting to happen."

"Don't knock it until we try it, Kai!" I replied. "Besides, I have a better idea. How about we combine it with the Neuro-Linguistic Paralyzer? We can paralyze them with laughter while they slip on the banana peels! It'll be the ultimate distraction!"

"Or a complete disaster," Delver interjected, adjusting his glasses as he peered into a nearby clutter of gadgets. "We're not even sure how the Neuro-Linguistic Paralyzer works yet."

"Details, details!" I waved my hand dismissively. "Let's just focus on the fun part! Who wants to volunteer to test the banana peel?"

"I'll do it!" Atticus piped up, raising his hand like a kid eager to answer a question in class. "As long as we have a soft landing area."

"You mean like the giant pile of soft marshmallows in the corner?" Akuma raised an eyebrow, clearly skeptical.

"Exactly!" Atticus grinned. "I'll be bouncing around like a human cannonball. Just don't forget to prepare the glitter!"

With that, we set to work, mixing ingredients, testing gadgets, and trying to figure out how to turn a perfectly good banana into a weapon of mass hilarity. We blended the Neuro-Linguistic Paralyzer with our banana peel formula, resulting in a concoction that looked suspiciously like a fruit smoothie gone rogue.

"Okay, smoothie in hand," I announced. "Now, who wants to activate the 'Laughter Inducer' button?"

"I'll take one for the team," Atticus said, puffing out his chest like a noble knight about to slay a dragon. "If I get paralyzed, just know that I did it for science."

"Or for the glory of exploding bananas!" Delver added with a chuckle.

We all gathered around as Atticus took a deep breath and squeezed the banana peel smoothie into the Neuro-Linguistic Paralyzer's control panel. A few sparks flew, the lights flickered, and suddenly, a bright beam of energy shot out, engulfing Atticus in a shimmering glow.

"Here goes nothing!" he shouted, before tossing the now-glittering banana peel onto the floor. It landed with a squishy thunk, and for a brief moment, we all held our breath.

Then, as if on cue, Atticus slipped on the banana peel, flailing his arms in slow motion as he spiraled downwards. For a moment, time froze. His face registered pure shock, and it felt like we were watching a blockbuster movie in slow motion.

"Why does this always happen to me?" he yelled, arms flailing as he hit the pile of marshmallows with an impressive splat.

The moment his body landed, the banana peel released a blast of glittery energy, enveloping Atticus in a cloud of sparkles while the Neuro-Linguistic Paralyzer kicked in. A wave of laughter erupted from all of us, and soon we were doubled over, clutching our stomachs as Atticus lay in the marshmallow pile, glimmering like a disco ball.

"Success!" I declared, wiping a tear from my eye. "Behold, the first-ever Neuro-Linguistic Paralyzer Banana Peel of Hilarity! The perfect weapon against boredom—and aliens!"

"That's great and all, but do you think it will actually work against aliens?" Akuma asked, trying to regain her composure.

"Well, it's worth a shot," I shrugged. "But if it doesn't, at least we can claim we've created the most absurd distraction in the galaxy!"

The room burst into laughter again, and for a moment, it felt like we had something special: a wacky invention that could bring joy to the darkest of times. We might have been facing a war with aliens, but at least we could throw a banana party while doing it.

With that, we returned to our brainstorming, our spirits lifted, and the tension in the room lightened by the absurdity of our invention. Little did we know, the aliens were still out there, plotting their next move while we were busy preparing for an all-out banana showdown.

As we basked in the glory of our ridiculous invention, a loud klaxon suddenly pierced the air, shattering our merry atmosphere like a glass ornament at a toddler's birthday party.

"Uh-oh," Akuma said, her voice dripping with sarcasm. "I think the universe is telling us to cut back on the banana jokes."

The alarm blared again, and a holographic screen flickered to life in the center of the lab, illuminating our faces in a ghostly glow. The screen displayed a series of blinking red dots, which I quickly recognized as the alien reconnaissance drones we had been expecting.

"Oh, great! Just what we needed—flying disco balls of doom," I muttered, grabbing a nearby banana peel and shoving it in my pocket for good measure. You never know when you'll need one!

Atticus, still slightly glittery from his marshmallow mishap, leapt to his feet. "Looks like it's showtime! Time to put our creation to the test!"

"Let's not forget the fact that these drones are probably armed to the teeth," Delver said, adjusting his glasses, which had somehow ended up on the back of his head. "Maybe we should focus on getting to safety first?"

"Safety is overrated! We've got bananas!" I declared, my voice a tad too enthusiastic. "Besides, I'd rather face a hundred alien drones with a banana in hand than hide behind a pile of marshmallows!"

"Only you would say that, Eleanor," Kai remarked dryly, rolling his eyes as he readied his own gadget—a high-tech slingshot that could launch everything from rocks to fully loaded marshmallows. "Let's just make sure we're not the ones getting shot at first."

With a renewed sense of purpose (and a bit of insanity), we dashed to our designated battle station, which, ironically, was a heavily reinforced snack bar. It was a place of comfort, yet oddly prepared for war. Rows of marshmallows, dried fruits, and—of course—bananas were piled high. Talk about a health hazard!

"Alright, here's the plan," I said, rallying the troops like a slightly over-caffeinated general. "We'll create a distraction using the banana peel. Atticus, you launch the Neuro-Linguistic Paralyzer while Kai covers us with the slingshot. Akuma, you and Delver focus on repairing the drones, and I'll do... um... whatever it is I do best!"

"Which is?" Akuma asked, a smirk on her face.

"Impressively ridiculous tactics!" I replied, waving my hands dramatically. "Trust me, it's a thing!"

Just then, the screen showed one of the alien drones zooming in on our lab. It was a sleek, metallic monstrosity with glowing blue eyes that screamed, "I mean business."

"Let's hope it doesn't recognize our ridiculousness as a threat," I muttered under my breath.

Before I could finish my thought, the drone blasted the lab's entrance with a bolt of blue energy, leaving a sizzling hole that would make a great entrance for a dramatic escape—if only it hadn't just burned half of our snack supplies.

"Looks like they don't appreciate our culinary talents!" Atticus yelled, hurling a banana peel toward the drone. The peel skidded harmlessly beneath it, causing the drone to veer to the side in what could only be described as an attempted pirouette. I'm not sure if it was a malfunction or if the drone had just given up on life.

"Quick! Aim for the eyes!" I shouted, hoping my battle strategy was as sound as it was ridiculous.

Delver launched a marshmallow directly at the drone, and it collided with a satisfying splat. The drone shuddered, the blue lights flickering wildly, and I could have sworn I saw it roll its "eyes" in exasperation.

"Perfect!" I shouted. "Marshmallows—one of nature's greatest weapons!"

Akuma pulled out a wrench from her utility belt and grinned. "I've been waiting for a chance to use this!"

"Wait, you actually have a plan?" Kai asked, incredulous. "You never told me!"

"Sure I do!" she replied, charging toward the drone. "I'm going to make it wish it had never crossed paths with a human!"

With that, she swung the wrench, making contact with the drone, which emitted a high-pitched whine. The drone began to wobble in the air like a drunken bee, emitting sparks and smoke.

"Did you just modify the drone with a wrench?" Atticus gaped. "That's... kind of awesome."

"Thank you! Now let's take this thing down!" Akuma shouted, and with one final swing, she sent the drone crashing to the ground, where it landed with a resounding thud.

As we cheered, I felt a rush of exhilaration wash over me. We might have started with bananas and marshmallows, but look at us now—armed with innovation, teamwork, and a dash of insanity!

"Alright, who's next?" I asked, looking around at my comrades. "We've got a whole fleet of aliens to impress!"

"Or confuse," Delver added, adjusting his glasses. "At this rate, we're not just fighting them; we're giving them a real show."

"Exactly! Let's get ready for the next wave!" I declared, charging back toward the makeshift battlefield. "This is going to be a hilarious war!"

The klaxon blared again, and I grinned. It wasn't just a battle; it was our battle. And if it meant unleashing our wild, banana-fueled chaos on the universe, then I was all in.

CHAPTER TWENTY-ONE

The Great Snack Standoff

If there's one thing I've learned about intergalactic warfare, it's that nothing brings people (and aliens) together quite like a good snack-off. So, when the second wave of drones descended upon our lab like angry hornets, I knew we were in for a treat. Literally.

"Prepare for battle!" I shouted, gripping a marshmallow catapult that Delver had rigged up. It was about as reliable as a high-school science project but way more fun.

"Do we have a plan this time?" Akuma asked, adjusting her protective goggles, which made her look like an overly enthusiastic mad scientist.

"Of course we do! We're going to make them regret their life choices!" I declared, twirling a banana like a baton. "And then we'll show them the ultimate human snack experience!"

"Great plan," Delver said, rolling his eyes but smirking. "So, do we lead with the marshmallows or the banana peel?"

"Both! But in that order," I replied, as if I had just discovered the secrets of the universe. "First, we soften them up with marshmallows, then we hit them with the banana peel distraction."

"Genius," Atticus said, standing beside me and flexing like he was about to bench-press the entire drone army. "Let's make this a snack to remember!"

The klaxon blared again as the drones approached, and I felt a rush of adrenaline. We were facing what seemed like a dozen alien drones, all hovering menacingly with their blinking lights and laser weapons. It was like the universe had decided to throw a really intense birthday party for the worst possible guests.

"Alright, team! On my count!" I raised my hand, feeling like a general ready to lead my troops into the chaos of culinary combat. "Three... two... one... marshmallow attack!"

With synchronized enthusiasm, we launched the marshmallows toward the approaching drones. They soared through the air like fluffy missiles, making delightful popping sounds as they hit their targets.

"Direct hit!" Kai cheered, tossing a few of his own. "These marshmallows are like meteorites of sweetness!"

"More like sugar bombs of doom!" Akuma shouted, launching her wrench with impressive accuracy. It ricocheted off a drone's exterior, causing it to spin wildly, like a dog chasing its tail but significantly more dangerous.

"Hey, look!" I yelled, pointing at the drone that had gotten knocked off-course. "It's trying to dance! I think we're onto something here!"

As we peppered the drones with sweets, one particularly ambitious alien drone swooped low, its laser blaring in warning. It was ready to fire, and I could practically see its angry little robot face glaring at us.

"Oh no you don't!" I shouted, ducking just in time. I whipped out a banana peel, holding it like a secret weapon. "You want to mess with us? Try slipping on this!"

With all the grace of a ninja on roller skates, I tossed the banana peel directly in its path. The drone hit the peel, spun out of control, and crashed into a pile of marshmallows. It was a glorious explosion of fluffiness!

"Banana slip!" I cheered, pumping my fist in victory. "Who knew they could be so effective in combat?"

"Careful, Eleanor! You might make a name for yourself as the 'Banana Bomber!'" Atticus called out, barely keeping his laughter in check as he aimed a marshmallow catapult.

"Hey, it's better than being the 'Marshmallow Magician,'" I shot back, loading up for another round. "At least bananas have potassium!"

Before I could fire another round, a series of holographic alerts flickered in the air. The drones were regrouping, their robotic voices crackling through the speakers.

"Warning: human snackage detected. Engaging countermeasures," one of them announced.

"Oh boy, that sounds serious," I said, raising an eyebrow. "But can they really counter marshmallows and banana peels? I mean, how do you even counter a snack?"

As if to answer my question, the drones activated what looked like tiny flamethrowers. "Warning: human snacks are highly flammable. Initiating burn protocol."

"Time to improvise!" Delver shouted, fumbling to adjust his slingshot. "Akuma, do you still have that wrench?"

"Always!" she said, brandishing it like a sword. "Time to give them a lesson in human ingenuity!"

With renewed determination, we began throwing whatever we could find—marshmallows, bananas, even a few snack packs that had survived the earlier chaos. It was the most ridiculous battle I had ever participated in, and oddly enough, it was also the most exhilarating.

The drones, flustered by our unconventional tactics, began to malfunction, their circuits sparking and blinking in confusion.

"Look! They can't handle our snack attacks!" I laughed, dodging a stray laser beam. "We're giving them a taste of chaos!"

"Or a taste of sugar overload," Atticus added, his voice rising above the chaos. "At this rate, they're going to need a dentist!"

Finally, after what felt like an eternity of flying snacks and chaotic laughter, we managed to send the last drone crashing into the snack bar. The explosion sent marshmallows flying in all directions, and I couldn't help but let out a whoop of joy.

"We did it!" I exclaimed, raising my banana in triumph. "We defeated the alien drones with the power of snacks!"

Delver surveyed the wreckage, his eyes gleaming with excitement. "I think we've just discovered the ultimate weapon against our enemies: pure absurdity."

As we celebrated, the alarm stopped blaring, and we took a moment to catch our breath. Marshmallow fluff coated our clothes, and the scent of burnt sugar wafted through the air.

"Alright, team! What's next on our agenda?" I asked, grinning widely. "Should we try to negotiate with the aliens? Maybe barter some marshmallows for peace?"

"Or we could invite them over for snacks!" Akuma suggested, her voice dripping with mock seriousness. "Who doesn't love a good banana split?"

We all burst out laughing, the tension of battle melting away like butter on hot toast. In that moment, it didn't matter how many aliens we faced or what crazy inventions we had up our sleeves; what mattered was that we were in this together, armed with snacks and a healthy dose of humor.

"Alright, snack warriors! Let's prepare for our next move!" I declared, raising my banana once more. "Who's ready to take on the universe?"

With our makeshift snack arsenal at the ready, we regrouped in the lab, which now resembled a scene from a food fight movie—if that movie had been directed by someone on a sugar high. Marshmallows were stuck to the ceiling, and a rogue banana peel had somehow found its way into Delver's hair, giving him a rather unfortunate hairstyle that we couldn't help but giggle at.

"Seriously, Delver," Akuma teased, trying to hold back her laughter. "Are you trying to channel a tropical vibe or are you just auditioning for a role as a fruit bowl?"

"Very funny, Akuma," Delver grumbled, trying to dislodge the banana peel from his hair while also attempting to maintain some semblance of dignity. "Maybe I'm just getting in touch with my inner smoothie."

"Smoothies are for losers!" I retorted, snickering as I handed him a marshmallow to throw at Akuma. "You're a snack warrior now! Embrace the chaos!"

"Can't we embrace the chaos with a little less... banana?" Delver replied, plucking the offending fruit from his head and tossing it aside. "At least until we figure out what the aliens are planning next."

"Good point," Atticus chimed in, stretching his arms above his head. "What do we know about these drones? I mean, besides the fact that they're really bad at dodging snacks?"

"Well," Akuma said, pulling up a holographic display that looked like it had seen better days, "the drones seem to have some sort of programming flaw. They can't counter human snacks effectively. We should exploit that."

"Snacks as a strategy?" I laughed, clapping my hands together. "This is going to go down in history. 'The Great Snack War of 2024: When Humanity Defeated Drones with Marshmallows!'"

"Sounds like a title for a bestselling novel," Delver mused. "But let's not forget that these drones are just the start. We need to prepare for the actual aliens. They're probably watching us right now, taking notes on our snacking strategy."

"Like they have any room to talk," Akuma scoffed. "What kind of race invades other planets with robots instead of snacks? Seriously, who does that?"

"Probably the same kind that refuses to trade recipes," I replied. "If we meet them, I'm definitely bringing a banana pie as a peace offering."

"Only if it's made with extra marshmallows," Atticus said, a mischievous glint in his eye. "We can start an intergalactic culinary festival. 'Welcome to

Earth, Where the Snacks are Out of This World!'"

"Now you're talking!" I grinned. "Let's just make sure the aliens know we're serious. If they want to pick a fight, they're going to have to do it over a plate of nachos."

Just then, our holographic display flickered, and a new alert popped up, indicating an incoming message from the central command of our faction. I hurriedly tapped the screen, and a familiar face appeared—a fellow member of our faction, looking as serious as a cat at a dog park.

"Team! We have a situation!" he said, his eyes wide with urgency. "We've received intel that more alien drones are on their way to our location, and they're bringing a new kind of weapon."

"Do they really think they can outsnack us?" I shot back, trying to keep the mood light, despite the tension in the air.

"Uh, this isn't a joke," the guy said, looking confused. "They've deployed drones equipped with food-repelling shields and—"

"Food-repelling shields?!" Akuma interrupted. "Why not just use a giant salad or something? They clearly don't understand the beauty of snack food!"

"Or the glorious fusion of flavors," I added, shaking my head. "The aliens are missing out on so much."

"Focus, people!" the guy exclaimed, his patience wearing thin. "We need a strategy before they arrive. What do we do?"

"Simple!" I exclaimed, feeling a burst of inspiration. "We turn their food-repelling shields against them!"

"Uh, how do we do that?" Delver asked, scratching his head. "Do we throw a giant salad at them?"

"No, you genius!" I said, smirking. "We're going to create a snack bomb. Something so delicious and irresistible that it will breach their defenses! If they think they can repel food, they've got another thing coming!"

"What's a snack bomb?" Atticus inquired, his brows furrowing.

"It's a bomb made of snacks, obviously! We can layer different types of food and create an explosion of flavor!" I explained, feeling the excitement bubble up inside me. "Imagine marshmallows, chocolate, bananas, and maybe some sour gummies for good measure."

"Now you're speaking my language," Delver said, his eyes lighting up. "I'm in!"

"Alright! Let's get to work!" I shouted, rallying the team. "If we can outsmart their food-repelling shields with sheer deliciousness, we'll send those aliens packing with their robotic tails between their legs!"

As we hurried to gather ingredients, I couldn't help but chuckle at the absurdity of our situation. Here we were, preparing to go to war with a snack bomb, all while trying to avoid being blasted to bits by alien drones. It was like something straight out of a bizarre comedy film.

"Alright, team! Gather all the supplies you can find! We're going to make history!" I called out, a determined glint in my eye. "And if we succeed, we'll become legends—the Snack Avengers of Earth!"

The team rallied, rushing around the lab like it was a frantic cooking show where the timer was counting down, and we were on the brink of culinary greatness. The clock was ticking, and so was our chance to outwit our alien foes with the power of snacks.

CHAPTER TWENTY-TWO

The Snack Bomb Countdown

The atmosphere in the lab had shifted. The once chaotic energy of marshmallows and giggles had transformed into something heavier, more electric. I stood at the center of our makeshift assembly line, the air thick with anticipation and the faint aroma of melted chocolate. The countdown had begun, and time felt like a tightrope walker balancing on a thread—one misstep, and we would plummet into chaos.

"Okay, team!" I called out, trying to keep my voice steady despite the butterflies flapping around in my stomach. "We're less than thirty minutes from the arrival of the drones. It's time to finalize the Snack Bomb."

As if on cue, a holographic display flickered to life, showcasing a countdown timer that felt as ominous as a ticking bomb—ironically, that's exactly what it was. The clock read 29:59, and I could practically hear the gears grinding in my head.

"Right, let's do a quick inventory check," Atticus said, his face suddenly serious. "We need to ensure we have enough firepower—uh, I mean, snack power—to breach those shields."

"Chocolate? Check." I pointed to a giant bowl of melted chocolate that was precariously balanced on the edge of the table. "Marshmallows? Double check. Gummy bears?" I scanned the area, and my heart sank. "Where are the gummy bears?!"

Delver was rummaging through a bag of snacks on the other side of the lab. "I think I saw them in the corner next to the chip bags!" he shouted back.

"Why on Earth would you put gummy bears next to chip bags?" Akuma exclaimed, tossing her hair over her shoulder with exaggerated annoyance. "That's like putting cats and dogs in the same room and expecting them to get along!"

"Focus!" I said, trying to keep the mood from getting too heavy. "We're in a war, remember? Snacks are vital!"

"Right, right!" Delver returned, arms laden with various snacks, including a slightly squished pack of gummy bears that looked like they had seen better days. "I found them! But uh, they might need a little... reconstitution."

I grimaced but grabbed the pack. "We'll make it work. Everyone grab your ingredients! We're down to twenty-five minutes!"

As we scrambled to prepare, the reality of our situation started to sink in. I could feel the tension creeping back in, coiling around my chest like a snake ready to strike. This wasn't just a food fight; we were about to go head-to-head with alien drones that could wipe us out with a single pulse of energy. The weight of our mission loomed over us, and I could almost hear the ominous ticking of the clock echoing in my ears.

"Alright, let's assemble the bomb," I directed, trying to keep my voice upbeat despite the rising stakes. "Layer by layer, like a weird culinary lasagna of doom!"

"More like a lasagna of potential disaster," Akuma said, rolling her eyes but smiling slightly as she poured melted chocolate over the marshmallows.

"Yeah, a lasagna that's probably going to explode in our faces," Delver joked, but his grin faded as he glanced toward the window. "But at least it will be a delicious explosion, right?"

The holographic timer ticked down to 20:00, and I couldn't help but feel the pressure mounting.

"Okay, here's the plan," I said, rallying my troops. "Once we finish the bomb, we'll launch it at the incoming drones. If they can't repel our snacks, we'll incapacitate them, and then we can take them down one by one!"

"Sounds like a solid plan," Atticus agreed, his expression fierce. "But what if the bomb doesn't work? We need a backup."

"Backup?" I scratched my head, my mind racing. "Uh, we could always make more snack bombs? Or we could resort to the age-old art of throwing food. You know, the classic 'hurl and hope' technique!"

"Now that's a battle strategy I can get behind," Delver chuckled, but his laughter faded as the holographic display flashed with a new alert. "Uh, guys? We have a problem."

My heart sank as I turned to face the screen. The map of our territory was lighting up with red dots, indicating the approaching alien drones, and the timer now read 15:30. They were almost here.

“Time to get serious, Snack Avengers,” I said, steeling myself. “We don’t have much time. Let’s finish this bomb and prepare for battle!”

The urgency surged through the lab as we threw ourselves into the task, layering chocolate, marshmallows, gummy bears, and whatever else we could find into a towering snack bomb that somehow managed to look both delicious and terrifying.

“Ten minutes!” Akuma shouted as she hastily piled on the last layer of gummy bears, which now resembled a sugar-coated fortress.

“Quick, someone grab the launch mechanism!” I yelled, scanning the chaotic scene for the potato cannon we had repurposed for this very occasion.

“Right here!” Atticus replied, brandishing the cannon like it was Excalibur. “Ready for action!”

With the bomb loaded and the launch mechanism in place, we gathered around the cannon like it was the Holy Grail of snack warfare. The countdown timer read 05:00, and adrenaline surged through my veins.

“On my mark, we fire!” I shouted, my heart racing. “Three... two... one...”

The timer flashed its final countdown as we all shouted in unison, “Snack bomb, GO!”

I pressed the trigger, and with a loud whoosh, the snack bomb launched from the cannon, soaring through the air like a bizarre meteor of delicious chaos. Time seemed to slow as we all watched, breathless, as it arced toward the incoming swarm of alien drones.

The snack bomb sailed through the air like a sweet comet, trailing a rainbow of sprinkles and melted chocolate behind it. I swear I could hear the sweet chorus of angels (or maybe just Akuma squealing) as it approached the alien drones, their metallic forms glinting ominously in the midday sun.

“Direct hit!” Atticus yelled, pumping his fist in the air.

But the moment of triumph was short-lived. As the bomb exploded in a glorious splash of confectionery chaos, showering the drones with marshmallows and gummy bears, the drones seemed to shake it off like a pesky fly. Instead of collapsing in sugary defeat, they retaliated with high-pitched whirrs, and a series of mechanical arms sprang forth, shaking off the candy like a dog emerging from a pool.

“Well, that’s... less effective than I hoped,” I muttered, watching in horror as the drones regrouped, their surfaces still shining ominously beneath the candy coating.

"Uh, guys?" Delver squeaked, backing away slowly. "I think they're mad. Really mad."

"Maybe they just need a little more snack therapy," I suggested, trying to lighten the mood, but no one was laughing. Instead, panic was palpable, a thick fog of anxiety swirling around us.

"Okay, retreat time!" I shouted, waving my arms like a windmill in a hurricane. "Back to the lab!"

We scrambled back inside, slamming the door shut behind us just as the drones began to converge on our position, their metallic wings buzzing like angry hornets.

"Do we have a plan B?" Akuma asked, her face pale as she leaned against the wall.

"Um, maybe we can bribe them with snacks?" I suggested weakly, knowing full well that it sounded as ridiculous as it felt. "Or we could throw more food at them until they surrender?"

"I vote for plan C: run away!" Delver said, his voice trembling. "Because I don't want to end up as a snack for the alien invaders!"

"Okay, okay!" I said, shaking my head to clear my thoughts. "Let's think logically. We have to outsmart these metal munchers."

"Do you have a genius plan?" Atticus asked, raising an eyebrow. "Because 'throwing snacks' isn't exactly a military strategy."

I paced back and forth, the wheels in my brain turning like a hamster on a wheel. "Alright, let's regroup. We need to find a way to distract them long enough to think of something."

Suddenly, an idea struck me. "What if we create a decoy? Something that looks like the snack bomb but doesn't explode! Just enough to lure them away while we think of a real plan."

"I love it!" Akuma exclaimed, her eyes sparkling with newfound determination. "But what are we going to use?"

"Anything that looks delicious," I said, my mind racing. "Chocolate bars, cookies—anything we can grab that looks remotely edible! It just needs to be shiny enough to catch their attention!"

"Let's do this!" Atticus said, rallying the troops. "We can assemble our snack decoy faster than they can process sugar!"

With renewed vigor, we dashed back to the assembly line, gathering whatever sugary items we could find. It was a frantic race against time, with the ominous drone buzz growing louder outside.

"Ten seconds!" I shouted, throwing a handful of chocolate chips into the decoy. "Make it count!"

As we layered more snacks, the timer on the wall glowed ominously, reflecting our dwindling time. "Five seconds!" Delver shouted, his voice rising in pitch. "Hurry!"

"Done!" I declared triumphantly just as the door shuddered under the weight of the drones.

"Get ready to launch!" Atticus positioned the decoy in the potato cannon, sweat glistening on his brow.

With a quick countdown from three, we fired the decoy into the air. It soared like a dream, trailing a glittering stream of sugary goodness that would make even Willy Wonka jealous.

"Go, decoy, go!" I cheered, my heart racing as the decoy flew off, attracting the drones like moths to a flame.

"Look! It's working!" Akuma shouted, pointing out the window. The drones swerved and began to chase the decoy, completely ignoring us.

"I can't believe that actually worked," I breathed, a mixture of relief and disbelief flooding my system.

But as I turned to celebrate with my friends, a loud crash echoed through the lab. The door buckled under the pressure of a drone that had broken through, its sensors glowing ominously as it zoomed toward us.

"Uh-oh," Delver said, his eyes wide as saucers.

"Scatter!" I yelled, and we all bolted in different directions.

In the chaos, I dove behind a table, narrowly avoiding the drone's metallic claws. "We need something to fight back with!" I shouted, searching the nearby shelves for anything that could help.

"More snacks!" Akuma yelled from the corner, tossing chocolate bars at the drone as if they were grenades. "Take that, you overgrown tin can!"

"Brilliant plan!" I called back sarcastically, but desperate times called for desperate measures.

"Okay, I'm going to try to short-circuit it!" Atticus shouted, holding up a bag of gummy bears. "Let's see if this works!"

He hurled the bag at the drone, and it exploded upon impact, covering the drone in a sticky layer of gummy goodness. The drone sputtered and sparked, temporarily blinded by the sugary chaos.

"Keep it busy!" I shouted, my heart racing. "I have an idea!"

I darted toward the control panel, frantically typing in commands. If I could just override its system...

"Come on, come on!" I muttered under my breath, my fingers flying over the keys. With one final keystroke, I hit enter, and the screen flashed green.

"Yes! I did it!" I yelled, and the drone suddenly stopped mid-air, hovering in confusion.

"Did you just hack it?" Delver gaped at me. "That's amazing!"

"More like a desperate attempt at survival," I laughed, but the tension was still thick in the air.

"Can you control it?" Akuma asked, her eyes wide with excitement.

"I think so!" I grinned, and with a flick of my wrist, the drone turned and zipped back outside, heading straight for the other drones chasing our decoy.

We watched in awe as it began to unleash a series of sparks and flashing lights, confusing the drones further.

"Looks like we turned the tide," Atticus said, grinning.

But I knew this was only a temporary victory. The real war was yet to come, and our Snack Bomb might have bought us time, but we still needed a solid plan moving forward.

"Alright, team," I said, determination setting in. "Let's regroup and figure out our next move. We need to strategize for the real fight against the aliens.

"Snack warriors assemble!" Delver cheered, raising his arms in triumph.

And just like that, we began plotting our next adventure, with the sweet taste of victory—and gummy bears—still lingering in the air.

CHAPTER TWENTY-THREE

The Time-Stopper 5000

I woke up to the faint beeping of the lab's intercom, which sounded suspiciously like a malfunctioning toaster trying to sing show tunes. I had thought last night's escapade with the snack bomb was the peak of our inventive prowess, but after a good night's sleep (more like a series of dreams about alien marshmallows chasing me), I was ready to dive back into the madness of invention.

"Alright, team! Today we're going to make something epic," I declared, flinging the lab door open. "Forget snacks; we need something that screams 'super advanced sci-fi.'"

"Like a laser that shoots glitter?" Akuma suggested, her eyes sparkling with mischief.

"Okay, first off, that sounds dangerously close to a party favor. We need something that can actually help us in a fight," I replied, waving her off. "And glitter is the enemy of cleanliness, so let's steer clear of that."

"Wait!" Delver shouted, raising a finger as if he had just discovered the meaning of life. "What if we invent a device that can stop time? Like a Time-Stopper 5000! We could freeze the aliens in their tracks while we plan our next move!"

"Delver, that's brilliant!" I exclaimed, clapping him on the back so hard he nearly stumbled forward. "Time-stopping technology! It's like those superhero movies, but we actually get to be the heroes."

"Can we also get capes?" Atticus asked, already looking far too enthusiastic about the prospect of superhero fashion.

"No capes!" I insisted. "Remember what happened to that guy who wore a cape? Total disaster. We need functionality, not fashion statements. Now, let's get to work!"

We gathered around our trusty workbench, the cluttered surface covered in wires, gadgets, and a few remnants of the previous day's snack explosion. It was chaotic, but somehow, it was the beautiful chaos of our creation process.

"Alright, let's brainstorm how this time-stopper will work," I began, scribbling ideas on a nearby whiteboard. "We need a power source—something strong enough to create a time bubble."

"Maybe we can harness energy from those evolution stones we've been collecting?" Akuma suggested, her brow furrowing in thought.

"Or we could use a mini black hole," Atticus chimed in, holding up a glass jar filled with what looked like glittering water. "I found this in the lab; could be useful!"

"Pretty sure that's just soda," I said, rolling my eyes. "But I appreciate the effort. Let's stick to the evolution stones for now."

As we worked, the lab filled with a symphony of sounds: the whirring of machines, the clinking of metal, and the occasional explosion that I hoped was merely a small mishap and not a precursor to an apocalypse.

"We'll need a way to activate the device," I said, my mind racing. "Maybe we can use a special button that, when pressed, will trigger the time stop."

"Let's make it dramatic!" Delver suggested, his eyes gleaming. "How about we create a huge red button that says 'DO NOT PRESS' on it? That way, when we press it, it'll feel like we're breaking all the rules of time and space!"

"That's genius!" Akuma replied, already sketching out designs for the button. "And we can make it light up and everything!"

"Okay, now we're cooking with gas!" I exclaimed, as the ideas began to flow like a river of creativity. "Let's get to work on this Time-Stopper 5000!"

Hours flew by in a flurry of activity, and soon enough, we had a prototype: a sleek device with glowing panels, a central sphere that housed our evolution stones, and—of course—the dramatic red button that screamed "DO NOT PRESS."

"Ladies and gentlemen, I present to you the Time-Stopper 5000!" I announced, striking a pose as if I were unveiling a fancy car at a showroom.

Delver clapped excitedly, and Akuma's eyes sparkled with pride. "What now? Should we test it?"

"Of course!" I said, eyeing the timer on the wall. "Let's see how much time we can stop! I'm going to press it—right after I think this through."

"Just press the button!" Atticus urged, practically bouncing on his toes.

"Okay, okay! On the count of three," I said, gathering everyone around. "One... two... three!"

I slammed my hand down on the red button. A brilliant flash of light erupted from the device, and suddenly, everything froze.

The buzzing of the machines halted, droplets of water hovered mid-air, and Delver was caught mid-sneeze, his face scrunched up in a bizarre expression that I would definitely be immortalizing in a future meme.

"Whoa! It worked!" I shouted, looking around at the frozen tableau.

"Can we move?" Akuma asked, her eyes wide with wonder.

"Only if we want to break the rules of time!" I said, waving my hands like a kid who just discovered a magical world. "We're in a time bubble! We can't leave this moment!"

"Let's take selfies!" Delver suggested, his face lighting up in excitement.

"Perfect!" I replied, whipping out my phone. "Strike a pose, everyone!"

We spent what felt like an eternity taking goofy selfies and exploring the frozen lab. I made funny faces, Delver did his best model impression, and Akuma posed dramatically next to a stack of cardboard boxes.

But as much as I loved our mini adventure, I knew we couldn't stay frozen forever. "Alright, we should probably unfreeze everything before someone starts wondering why we're missing," I said reluctantly.

"Agreed," Atticus said, eyeing the timer on the wall that read "00:00."

"Okay, here goes nothing!" I said, pressing the button again.

Another flash of light engulfed us, and suddenly everything whirled back to life, the world resuming its usual chaos.

"Whoa, did we just freeze time?" Delver asked, looking around in awe.

"Yup, and it was glorious!" I said, grinning from ear to ear.

"Can we use it to stop the aliens?" Akuma asked, her eyes gleaming with excitement.

"Absolutely," I replied. "But let's keep this as a last resort. We don't want to accidentally create a time loop or something. I'm still recovering from our last snack fiasco."

With our Time-Stopper 5000 in hand, I felt a surge of confidence. We were now armed with something that could potentially turn the tide in our favor. But in the back of my mind, I knew that we were still racing against time, and the real war was just around the corner.

"Let's get back to work!" I declared, determination settling in as I glanced at my friends. "The aliens won't know what hit them!"

As we returned to our blueprints, the air buzzed with a sense of purpose. With our new invention, we might just stand a chance against whatever cosmic chaos was coming our way.

With our Time-Stopper 5000 buzzing softly on the workbench, I felt a surge of optimism. I mean, what could go wrong? Time manipulation was totally in my wheelhouse, right? Right.

"Okay, so we've got the time-stopping device," I said, rubbing my hands together. "Now we need to figure out how to use it strategically. We can't just go around freezing time for fun and selfies. Well, maybe one more selfie." I lifted my phone, grinning like an overexcited child.

"Why not? We could freeze the aliens mid-invasion, take a selfie, and then unfreeze them just to watch their confused faces," Akuma suggested, barely suppressing a laugh.

"Brilliant, but I'm not sure the aliens would appreciate our humor. Plus, I'm pretty sure they'd be less than thrilled about being in a selfie with a bunch of humans," I said, snickering at the mental image. "They'd probably be all, 'What is this weird ritual?'"

"Hey, maybe we can start an intergalactic meme page!" Delver chimed in, his eyes wide with excitement. "The first post could be of them mid-yell. 'When you realize the humans just took a selfie instead of fighting back!'"

"Now you're thinking like a true strategist," I said, giving him a thumbs-up. "But in all seriousness, we need to plan for actual usage. We've got to think of scenarios where freezing time would give us a significant advantage. And not just for memes, even if they are glorious."

As we dove deeper into brainstorming, the atmosphere shifted from lighthearted banter to serious strategizing. Delver suggested a range of scenarios, from ambushing aliens to stopping important meetings before they could escalate into full-on chaos.

"Imagine if we could freeze a whole negotiation session," Delver said, his voice animated. "We could slip in some ridiculously funny demands—like mandatory naptime for all aliens. 'You can't invade our planet until you've had your rest!'"

"That sounds like a winning strategy," Atticus chuckled, nodding in agreement. "But let's not forget about the potential backlash. The aliens might decide that our planet is full of crazies, and who could blame them?"

Just as we were reveling in our imaginary negotiations, an urgent beeping noise broke our concentration, sending my heart racing. I turned to the intercom, where a frantic voice crackled through.

"ATTENTION, ALL FACTIONS! URGENT MESSAGE FROM THE HIGH COMMAND! WE HAVE RECEIVED INTELLIGENCE ABOUT AN ALIEN SCOUTING PARTY IN OUR SECTOR! PREPARE FOR IMMINENT

ACTION!"

"Oh, great! Just when we thought we had a handle on things!" I exclaimed, running a hand through my hair. "Looks like it's showtime, team."

"Should we test the Time-Stopper 5000 in the field?" Akuma suggested, her eyes gleaming with excitement.

"Right! What better way to debut our shiny new toy than against actual aliens?" I said, trying to sound nonchalant even as my stomach twisted with nerves. "It's like a rite of passage for young inventors—except, you know, with real stakes."

We rushed to gather our gear, the mood shifting from playful to focused as we prepared for the mission. The Time-Stopper was secured in my backpack, and we donned our faction insignias, a mix of determination and adrenaline coursing through us.

"Okay, so what's the plan?" Atticus asked, checking his equipment with a seriousness that felt like it belonged in a movie trailer.

"Let's do a quick recon. We'll use our stealth skills—like ninjas but cooler," I replied, trying to channel my inner strategist. "We'll locate the scouting party, then decide if we want to freeze time, negotiate, or, you know, engage in some epic combat. But definitely no glitter!"

As we moved out, the tension in the air was palpable. I could almost hear the dramatic music swelling in the background. Our destination was a secluded area near the edge of the research facility, a hotspot for suspicious alien activity.

With each step, my heart raced faster. This wasn't just another day in the lab; we were stepping into the unknown, ready to face whatever challenges awaited us.

Arriving at our chosen spot, we crouched behind a pile of crates, our eyes scanning the area. The sun was setting, casting a warm glow over the landscape, and the shadows danced eerily.

"There they are!" Akuma whispered, pointing toward a group of aliens huddled around a small device. They were bizarre-looking, with bright colors that made them seem like they'd stepped straight out of a psychedelic dream.

"Okay, time to assess the situation," I said, peeking over the crates. "We can either sneak up and eavesdrop, or we can go full ninja mode and try to take them out."

"What if we freeze them and then eavesdrop?" Delver suggested, grinning like a maniac. "We could learn all their secrets while they're stuck mid-sentence."

"Tempting, but what if they explode or something?" I mused. "I'd rather not be caught in an alien fireworks show."

"Okay, let's do this smart. I'll activate the Time-Stopper, and we'll gather intel," I decided, my hands shaking slightly as I prepared the device. "Ready?"

"Ready!" everyone echoed, adrenaline coursing through our veins.

With a deep breath, I pressed the glowing button on the Time-Stopper 5000. The familiar flash of light enveloped us, and suddenly, the world around us froze. The aliens were mid-conversation, their eyes wide, and one of them was even in the middle of taking a sip from a shimmering drink.

"We're actually doing this," I said, grinning as I stepped into the frozen moment. "This is so cool!"

"Now let's snoop!" Akuma whispered, and we crept closer to the aliens, trying to stifle our giggles.

As we listened in, we learned about their plans—attempting to gather intelligence on our capabilities and weaknesses. It seemed they were trying to figure out how to conquer Earth, which wasn't exactly surprising, given the circumstances.

"Can you believe these guys?" I said, trying to keep my voice low as we exchanged incredulous looks. "They think they can just waltz in here and take over!"

"This just makes me want to win even more," Atticus said, eyes narrowing. "We can't let them succeed."

"Okay, but let's make it even more interesting," Delver suggested. "What if we prank them when we unfreeze time? Like, I don't know, give them a really loud noise to wake up to!"

"Now you're speaking my language!" I exclaimed, suppressing laughter. "Let's see how they handle a sudden flash mob of chaos!"

As we prepared for the grand reveal, I glanced back at the aliens, still frozen in time. This was going to be a moment to remember—a hilarious chapter in our ongoing war against the cosmos.

"On three," I said, my heart racing. "One... two... three!"

I pressed the button again, and time resumed. The aliens blinked, momentarily disoriented, as a burst of loud music erupted from my backpack, accompanied by blaring party horns and flashing lights.

The aliens jumped back, their wide eyes reflecting shock and confusion. "What is happening?!" one shouted, clearly bewildered.

We burst into laughter, the sight of bewildered aliens doing their best impression of startled cats sending us into fits of giggles.

"Let's get out of here!" I shouted, before we turned to dash back to our hiding spot, our laughter echoing through the air.

As we regrouped, I couldn't help but feel a sense of triumph. We might not have gotten into a full-on battle, but we had made our mark. With each step we took, it became clearer that our ingenuity and humor could be just as powerful as any weapon.

With a newfound determination, we set our sights on the next challenge. We were ready to face whatever the universe threw at us, one laugh and one time stop at a time.

CHAPTER TWENTY-FOUR

The Calm Before the storm

With our laughter still echoing in the air, we regrouped at the lab, high-fiving each other as we shared tales of our recent escapade. The aliens, now thoroughly confused by our unexpected antics, had decided to retreat—perhaps for a quick intergalactic therapy session. But little did we know that our time of playful pranks was coming to an end.

"Okay, team, that was fun, but we need to focus," I said, trying to pull my head out of the clouds. "We can't let our guard down. The aliens may be weirded out, but they're not done with us."

"Right," Akuma said, her eyes narrowed. "If they think they can just leave after that, they're in for a rude awakening."

"Exactly! We need to figure out what their next move will be. And if they think we're a bunch of jokers, it's only going to make things worse for them," I replied, bouncing on my toes, excitement bubbling beneath the surface.

Delver pulled up a holographic map of the surrounding area, his brow furrowed. "Let's analyze where they might be heading next. They've got to regroup somewhere to come up with a new plan."

As the map illuminated the lab, I scanned over it, adrenaline pumping through my veins. The thrill of the unknown danced in the air, but it was tinged with an ominous feeling that something big was on the horizon.

"Okay, so we've dealt with one scouting party," Atticus said, tracing a line on the map. "But if they're sending scouts, that means they're planning something larger—a full-scale attack. We need to be ready for anything."

Just as I was about to respond, an alert blared from the intercom, cutting through the chatter like a knife.

"ATTENTION! ALL FACTIONS! NEW INTELLIGENCE REPORT! WE HAVE DETECTED MULTIPLE ALIEN VESSELS HEADING TOWARD EARTH! THEY'RE NOT SLOWING DOWN!"

The room fell silent. My heart dropped as the implications of the announcement washed over us like a cold wave.

"Great," I said, my voice shaky. "Just when we thought we could catch our breath, the universe decides to throw a massive curveball."

"We knew they wouldn't back down for long," Akuma said, determination flashing in her eyes. "We've got to rally the factions and prepare for what's coming."

As we hurried to assemble our team, I felt a surge of anxiety mixed with excitement. This was it—the moment we had been preparing for. The Time-Stopper 5000 and our previous antics had merely been a warm-up.

"Let's put our plan into action," I said, trying to keep the energy high. "We've got research institutes, weapons, and each other. We're ready for whatever they throw our way."

With a new sense of purpose, we gathered our teams, briefing each faction on the impending alien invasion. The seriousness of the situation weighed heavily on us, but we also knew we had each other's backs.

Hours passed as we prepped, strategized, and gathered intel. The air was thick with tension, and the laughter we'd shared felt like a distant memory. Yet there was still a flicker of hope, a reminder of what we stood for.

"Alright, everyone!" I called out as we gathered for one last rally. "We're on the cusp of something huge. We've spent the last thousand years preparing, and now it's time to show the aliens what we're made of!"

Cheers erupted from the crowd, a unified roar of determination filling the air. But as the chants faded, I felt a chill run down my spine.

"Remember, they may have advanced technology, but we have something they don't: our will to fight and the element of surprise." I paused, scanning the faces of my friends, allies, and comrades. "We won't just be defending our planet; we'll be fighting for each other, for our families, and for every person who has ever doubted us!"

Suddenly, the lights flickered, and the intercom crackled again. "WE HAVE DETECTED ALIEN ACTIVITY IN THE ATMOSPHERE. INCOMING VESSELS APPROACHING AT HIGH SPEED!"

"Here we go!" Delver shouted, excitement and fear mixing in his voice.

"Remember the plan!" I shouted as we sprang into action, adrenaline surging. "Stick together, and don't forget to have fun! Wait, no—do forget to have fun! This is serious!"

As we sprinted to our positions, I couldn't shake the feeling that this was just the beginning. The aliens were coming, and with them, a battle unlike anything we'd ever faced.

The atmosphere crackled with anticipation, but deep down, I knew this would be a turning point—one that would lead us straight into the heart of a war that would determine the fate of Earth.

And as I looked up into the sky, watching the alien ships approach, I couldn't help but feel that we were on the brink of something monumental. Our time of preparation was over, and the war was about to begin.

But little did we know, the real battle was not just with the aliens but with ourselves—the choices we would make, the friendships we would forge, and the sacrifices we would have to face.

As the first alien ship broke through the clouds, I felt an icy grip of dread clutch my heart.

As we lined up for our battle stations, the tension in the air was palpable. It was as if someone had replaced all the oxygen with carbon dioxide, making it difficult to breathe without hyperventilating. I glanced around at my team—Atticus, Delver, Akuma, and the rest of our crew. We were all in it together, bound by the shared experience of the ridiculous situations we had encountered.

"Okay, team, we've trained for this," I said, trying to sound braver than I felt. "Let's put all that practice into action. Remember, we've faced crazier things than an alien invasion!"

"Like that time you tried to turn your old phone into a time machine?" Atticus quipped, grinning. "That was a real 'blast from the past!'"

"Hey! That phone had potential!" I shot back, trying to suppress a laugh. "Just because it ended up launching a full-on karaoke party doesn't mean it was a total failure!"

"Yeah, and you still owe me a round of 'Total Eclipse of the Heart' karaoke after that!" Delver chimed in, nudging me with a playful elbow.

As the banter flew, I felt a surge of confidence. If we could handle a karaoke crisis, we could definitely deal with aliens.

"Focus, people!" Akuma called out, trying to reign in our merriment. "We have an invasion to thwart! And no more karaoke until we win this war!"

The laughter quickly faded as the reality of the situation settled back in. Our research teams had been working tirelessly to gather intel, develop weapons, and devise a plan. But the impending alien attack hung over us like a black cloud ready to burst.

"Let's do a quick recap," I said, rallying everyone's attention. "We have our positions mapped out, the research institutes have fortified their defenses, and we know where those ships are likely to land."

"Right," Atticus added. "And remember, they might have technology we can't even comprehend yet. Stay sharp and keep your eyes peeled for any surprises."

Suddenly, the intercom blared, and a voice crackled through. "ATTENTION ALL FACTIONS! ALIEN SHIPS HAVE ENTERED EARTH'S ATMOSPHERE! PREPARE FOR IMMINENT CONTACT!"

I felt my stomach drop, and the lightheartedness we had just shared evaporated like mist in the morning sun. This was it—the moment we had been waiting for, but also dreading.

"We need to move!" I shouted, adrenaline surging through my veins. "Positions, now!"

We rushed to our assigned spots, and I could feel the pulse of the energy around us, charged with anticipation and fear. As I looked up, the sky was marred with shadows—massive alien vessels, sleek and ominous, descending from the clouds like harbingers of doom.

"Okay, guys, stay focused!" I reminded everyone. "We've got this. Just remember: if we can make it through an awkward school dance, we can face anything!"

As the first ship touched down, a shudder ran through the ground. My heart raced as the alien vessel opened, revealing a ramp that extended like the world's most dramatic staircase. And what emerged? A creature that looked like it had been designed by a committee of bad art students—tall, gangly, with eyes that were way too big and a mouth that seemed more suited for an anemone than an actual face.

"Uh, I didn't sign up for this!" Atticus whispered, nudging me as we squinted at the approaching aliens. "What are they even wearing? Is that a jumpsuit or a failed attempt at fashion?"

"Probably both," I muttered. "But they seem confident, which is more than I can say for us right now."

As they stepped closer, my heart thudded in my chest. "Remember your training! These are just aliens! They probably just want to study us and take our lunch money."

"Or maybe they'll want to challenge us to an intergalactic game of rock-paper-scissors," Delver joked, attempting to lighten the mood.

With a loud mechanical hiss, the alien leader, who looked like a cross between a praying mantis and an overly caffeinated chef, raised its appendage. "WE COME IN PEACE! AND FOR YOUR COOKIES!"

There was a beat of silence, and then a collective laugh erupted from our ranks.

"Wait, cookies?" Akuma said, raising an eyebrow. "Do they mean our actual cookies, or is this some sort of alien euphemism?"

"I mean, if they think we're giving them cookies for free, they've got another thing coming," I added, trying to suppress my grin.

But before we could indulge in more laughter, the alien leader cleared its throat. "NO COOKIES? THEN WE WILL TAKE OVER YOUR PLANET!"

"Guess we're fresh out of cookies, guys!" Atticus shouted dramatically. "We'd better get ready for a fight!"

The laughter faded again, replaced by the harsh reality that these aliens were not here for snacks—they were here for a war. I nodded, shaking off the nerves that crept up my spine.

"Let's show them what we're made of!" I shouted, rallying my friends. "We may be outnumbered, but we have something they don't: the element of surprise and a ridiculous amount of energy drinks!"

As the alien ships loomed ominously overhead, I couldn't shake the feeling that this was just the beginning. We had come too far to back down now. With our faction united and our wits about us, we charged forward, ready to defend our planet and protect what we held dear.

But as the first shot rang out and the battle commenced, I realized that while this was our moment of truth, it was also the prelude to something much larger.

We were on the cusp of war—one that would test our limits and challenge everything we thought we knew about ourselves, our alliances, and the power of humanity.

The stakes had never been higher, and the fight was only just beginning.

As we sprinted toward the chaos, I couldn't help but marvel at the absurdity of our situation. Here we were—students who had once worried about grades, homework, and whether or not the cafeteria would serve pizza again—and now we were preparing to face off against alien invaders demanding cookies. If only my high school English teacher could see me now.

The first shot rang out with a blinding flash of light, sending a jolt of adrenaline coursing through me. The aliens, with their praying mantis-like leader at the forefront, were launching energy blasts that looked like they belonged in a video game, not a real-life battle.

"Take cover!" I shouted, diving behind a nearby pile of alien tech that looked suspiciously like a giant disco ball.

"Great cover, Eleanor!" Akuma yelled from behind a nearby rock. "Nothing says 'stealth' like hiding behind a shiny orb!"

"I was hoping it would be a lucky charm!" I shot back, peeking around the edge to see the aliens regrouping.

As the chaos continued, I noticed that Atticus had whipped out his signature move: the Dance of Distraction. He began flailing his arms and legs in a wild attempt to catch the aliens' attention.

"Hey! Over here, you big bug-eyed losers!" he shouted, doing a little shimmy that looked more like a seizure than a dance.

"Why do you insist on embarrassing yourself?" Delver groaned, shaking his head. "This is a battle, not a talent show!"

"Every great leader has their unique style!" Atticus declared proudly, executing a particularly awkward spin. "They'll be so confused by my moves that they won't know what hit them!"

To my shock, the alien leader paused, its giant eyes blinking in what could only be described as confusion. I couldn't help but chuckle—Atticus was somehow winning the first round of psychological warfare with his ridiculous dance.

"See? It's working!" he shouted, glancing back at us with a triumphant grin.

"Don't get cocky!" Akuma yelled. "Keep the distractions coming! We need to buy time while we figure out a plan!"

As Atticus continued his unorthodox dance, I quickly scanned the battlefield. Our faction was trying to coordinate, but it was hard to keep a straight face with Atticus moonwalking like he was auditioning for an alien version of Dancing with the Stars.

"Okay, guys, focus!" I said, trying to sound serious despite the laughter bubbling in my chest. "We need a real plan. What are our options?"

"Why not just offer them cookies?" Delver suggested with a smirk. "It's clearly what they want!"

"Great idea! Except I think we might need a backup plan in case they don't have a sweet tooth," I replied, glancing around for anything we could use as a weapon.

Just then, I spotted our research institute's latest invention: the Overkill Cookie Cannon. It was a bizarrely massive contraption that looked like a cross between a cannon and a bakery. I had heard the engineers designed it to launch cookies at supersonic speeds.

"Okay, this is insane," I said, already plotting my next move. "But it might just work. Let's blast them with cookies!"

The rest of the team looked at me like I had just suggested we dance our way to victory. But desperation has a funny way of making even the craziest ideas sound reasonable.

"Alright, who's in charge of firing the cannon?" I asked, pointing at the absurd contraption. "And who's brave enough to reload it?"

"I'll do it!" Akuma volunteered, raising her hand. "I have a good aim! Plus, I love cookies!"

"I'm not sure that's the criteria we need right now," Delver pointed out, rolling his eyes.

"Look, we either distract them with cookies or dance moves!" I argued, half-laughing at the sheer ridiculousness of the situation. "Which sounds better?"

As the debate raged on, Atticus continued to dance, now incorporating some questionable breakdancing moves that sent a few aliens scratching their heads in confusion. Honestly, I half-expected them to join in any moment.

"Forget it! We're firing the cookie cannon!" I announced, moving toward the contraption. I quickly gathered a few bags of cookies from the nearby supply stash while Akuma rushed to the cannon.

"Load it up!" she called, grinning as she stuffed cookies into the cannon's mouth like a kid at a candy store.

"Now, aim it for maximum chaos!" I shouted. "Make sure we hit their leader first!"

With a final flourish, Akuma cranked the lever, and the cannon roared to life, shooting a barrage of cookies into the air. They soared like colorful missiles, raining down upon the aliens with surprising accuracy.

"Look out!" I yelled as one of the cookies hit the praying mantis leader square in the face, knocking its oversized antennae askew. The alien let out a shocked screech, flailing about as if it were trying to swat a pesky fly.

"Direct hit!" Delver cheered, fist-pumping the air.

As cookie carnage ensued, I realized that maybe our approach wasn't half bad. If we couldn't outsmart them, we might as well make them laugh. The battlefield became a frenzy of laughter, chaos, and cookie-dodging aliens.

With the aliens momentarily distracted, we seized the opportunity to regroup and strategize. But just as I felt a surge of confidence, a loud rumble echoed overhead.

"Uh-oh," I muttered, glancing up. "What's that?"

A colossal ship hovered above us, larger than any we had encountered before. It loomed ominously, casting a dark shadow over the battlefield.

"Um, guys, I think we've got company!" I said, feeling a lump form in my throat.

"Looks like the real war is about to begin," Akuma whispered, her earlier excitement fading.

With our goofy cookie-launching tactics still fresh in our minds, we stood on the precipice of something monumental. We had laughed and danced our way through the first encounter, but now it was time to face the consequences of our chaotic approach.

"Brace yourselves, everyone," I said, my heart pounding in my chest. "This isn't just a snack time anymore. We're about to find out if our ridiculousness can withstand an actual invasion."

As the alien ship descended and the tension mounted, I couldn't shake the feeling that we were teetering on the edge of something massive—a battle that would change everything.

And deep down, I knew that whatever awaited us next would test our courage, our resolve, and our ability to keep laughing in the face of danger.

But one thing was certain: we were ready to fight—and we were going to do it with style.

"This is it," I whispered, adrenaline coursing through me. "Welcome to the war."

Thank You For Reading <3

Hey pookies, I really hope you enjoyed edition 1 of the book, the next book will release by the end of January 2025, as always, I love you guys, and I'm very thankful you stuck around until the end Bye!

www.ingramcontent.com/pod-product-compliance
Lightning Source LLC
LaVergne TN
LVHW091325150826
845673LV00006B/1773

* 9 7 9 8 8 9 5 5 6 9 4 8 1 *